Falling Star

A NOVEL

H.B. Catherine

In loving memory of Bryan Shelly
February 1992-December 2009.
Gone, but never forgotten.
May your story live on & inspire others to never give up.

Acknowledgements

A wonderful thanks to my parents for always believing in me, and being there for me when I needed them. I'd also like to extend my gratitude to my Uncle Mark, Aunt Candy, Aunt Melissa, and my Grandpa Ernie for helping with this and to the other wonderful people who made this book possible, especially; Nicholas Farmer, Brian Butchbaker, Cal Noell, & Katie Marko-Bush. I am beyond grateful to everyone who contributed to making this a success.

Chapter 1

Sometimes, life can be hard. That seems to be the general consensus anyways. Life is not always picking flowers, carefree worries, and sappy love stories. Life is sometimes hard; it can be tragic; and it can be confusing. But, through all that, isn't it worth it? This crazy thing called life?

I suppose I should start this off by telling you that my name is Ella Cane. The majority of my friends call me El, or Ellie. That seems to be the norm nowadays, shortening names that are already rather short. It seems a bit silly to me, but I don't really mind. I suppose if I tried to get them to stop, they wouldn't anyway. It just seems to slip from their tongues.

Lets see, I guess that I am what is considered a "normal" teenager. I have that shaggy brown hair that looks similar to mud, but my mother is always trying to tell me that "is as golden as the sun." I decided to cut it all off last year. I think it broke her heart a little bit- I did feel quite badly for that. I am 18 years old now though, she should understand that I need to do things for me. It is my senior year of high school, who hasn't done something a bit crazy? But I digress; I also have mud brown eyes (still normally referred to as "golden") that matches my hair. I am average height, and average build. I play sports, and I get good grades. I am friends with most everyone, and I do what is expected of me most of the time. I know you must be thinking how average I seem and you are right. In the craziness that is the world today I am pretty average. But, here in this little town where I live, I am an original; a one of a kind.

Everyone knows my name, my family, my history. This little farm town in nowhere Michigan is the only place that I have ever known, the place I call home. Nothing new happens, and life goes on just fine. I can't wait to get out of this place as soon as I graduate. I am not sure where to yet. But as many things that I love about this town, I can't stay here.

How else should I start this, oh, perhaps the most important thing about my story is that it is not about me at all. I mean, I am aware that I am quite an intriguing individual, but no, this story is about my best friend. His name is Byron Rood. He is the boy that my life revolves around. In this little town, he gives me hope, and he makes me believe that anything is possible.

Byron is the boy that was never meant to be here in the first place, he is like an oddity put here by mistake. In a place full of normality, he radiates eccentricity. Take his looks for example. His hair is the black that shines so bright it seems almost blue. He grows it long, and every girl gazes in his direction as he walks past. His eyes are the darkest brown you've ever seen. Their hint of sparkle like pieces of Smoky Quartz. He is beautiful, almost ethereal.

Now, you may be thinking, he must be conceited, a beauty like this. But, that is another thing about him- he is humble and kind. He is that person who excels at everything he ever attempts. The kind of person most people can't help but like, as much as they want to hate him. For example, I have been competing with him for valedictorian since we hit freshman year. He seems to have a much easier time achieving A's than I do; a natural intelligence that infuriates me! But how can you hate someone who will stop at the drop of a hat to help you out, no questions asked, just because that same someone kicked your ass on the last Calculus test?

Yes, this is a story about a boy who was dumped on this earth, full of the life in a way that some of us never find. "Just another story about a boy?" you might ask. But this is not just a story about any boy. This tale is of my boy.

"Byron! Wait up! I want to walk to school with you!" I screech, as he slowly stops and waits for me. I can almost see the visible sigh his shoulders make, knowing that his quiet morning walk will more than likely be spoiled by my loud, rambunctious conversation. "Hey Byron, great morning for a walk to school right?" I breathlessly greet him, finally caught up.

"Good morning Ella. Yes it is… Even if it is only a short walk there." He finally turns to me, unable to control the chuckle that escapes him from looking at my flushed face and corny smile. "Yes, it is." He says again, as the happiness of my unplanned arrival registers in his gaze. It is always like that with him. As if my presence takes him a moment to decide if the company is wanted or not. Some days I know that my silence is preferred, but today, I know that my chatter is welcome.

"How are you doing today? Did you do the Calculus homework?"

"I'm good. Yes, I did. Do you need any help with it?" As he looks my way once more, with that mischievous gleam in his eye, knowing that I would have questions.

"Yes, I do. I just do not understand why we need to know this stuff! I will never use it. Will you help me with some problems before class? Ms. Keens never answers my questions."

"Yeah, I can help you during Spanish, I doubt we will be doing anything." He replies, knowing full well that we never do anything during Spanish class. Before I can chime in with a smart remark, we have reached the school, and my friends bombard me, ending the conversation.

"EL! Are you ready for the game today?!" My closest friend, Emily, screams in my direction, coming straight at us. Byron avoiding the unwanted attention, makes a run for his locker before the rest of my friends advance. This is a regular occurrence. I just give him the nod, and allow myself to be tackled by my group of friends.

"Yes, yes, I am ready! How about you guys?" I laugh at them, knowing that we are all ready for the game. My friends are quite the crazy bunch. I have known them all since we started school, and my family knew their families before that. Small town stuff, everyone knowing everyone. Emily has been my best friend since we were in kindergarten together, when we first discovered that we both enjoyed throwing rocks at the boys. She has that natural beauty, where no make up is necessary. Long straight dirty-blonde hair that is constantly being swept out of her face. Despite the differences in looks, she is the most like me of all of our friends. Shy and quiet (most of the time). Emily does have quite the temper though, especially when she is wrong.

My other two friends who skidded in on Emily's heels, are Tara and Samantha. Tara has the tendency to wear too much make up, but it looks good against her dark complexion and dark tangle of curls. But Samantha? She is the Barbie Doll. The leader of the group. What I mean by that is she is the one who can talk us all into pretty much any shenanigan. What am I saying. She can pretty much talk anyone into anything. She is the queen of the school. You know- the gorgeous blonde who has everything and confidence that makes the rest of us look like giant balls of insecurity? That is her, but I love her nonetheless. Together the four of us are inseparable. The school is at our feet.

"Of course we are! I have been practicing my free-throws all morning, I am on it. Though, Tara still needs a little work!" Samantha laughs, and nudges Tara, letting her know that it is just a joke (kind of). That is how we teenage females are, kind with just a hint of cruel at the same time.

"Did we scare away Byron?" Tara glares at Samantha, and changes the spotlight to me once more. Samantha continues to giggle, but this time, at my situation.

"Nooo, you just know how he is." I reply, rolling my eyes as they all poke me for information they think that I am withholding from them. You see, they all think that there is something going on between Byron and I. And, well, I wish there was, but sadly, nada. The boy has had me friend zoned since that first time I forced him to sit with me in band when we were 10 years old. That moment when I plopped myself next to him, and told him that these would be our seats from then on, I have to admit, he was a little annoyed. But he continued to sit by me. So, our odd friendship began.

"Oooh, Ellie, you are so smitten! It is written all over your face every time you are with him! Just admit it!" Emily chimes at me, daring me to take the bite.

"Emily, shut up. We are going to be late!" I retort, knowing that would get the gang moving and off the sensitive subject of my puppy love.

Giggling, we all head towards our first class; English. One of my favorite classes. I love writing. It is the place for me to go when I need to think, it calms me. Of course, I do not let any of my friends know this, I get mocked enough for my perfect grades and nerdy habits. It helps that I also like my teacher for this class. His name is Mr. Dwayne. He is the type of teacher that you respect, but are also slightly afraid of. His presence is domineering, but you learn a lot, well, at least I do. He also happens to be my track coach, so the fact that I enjoy running and writing bonds us. Most students he tends to give hell to, but we seem to have an unspoken understanding: I continue to run and get good grades, he lets me space out in class from time to time.

Today is one of those days where I just need to let my mind roam. Mr. Dwayne begins the class on the paperback we were supposed to have read today, which means, that we are going to spend the majority of class rereading it aloud because I am one of the only people who actually did the assignment outside of class. This, especially today, is a plus for me. I have a lot to think about. I have my basketball game against our rival school tonight, no slip ups, especially since we play after the boys' team. Our boys' team is very good, they have not lost a game yet. It is quite intimidating, considering that Byron is the lead point guard. I can't seem to match his skill on the court, or even in the classroom. The boys enjoy watching our game, and we enjoy watching theirs. Our team is not undefeated, but we are decent. It helps that occasionally we practice with the guys.

Focus, Ella! I think loudly at myself. I really need to start going over the plays in my head before this game, so I do not forget them. My brain tends to get sidetracked rather easily, especially when it comes to Byron. Gosh, I am pathetic. No one really knows how pathetic I am though, I mean, my friends have an idea of course, but I prefer to keep my feelings in check.

You see, Byron is not only my best friend, but something more. When I am around him, I cannot help but radiate. I love him, and not just the, *"Oh giggle, giggle, he is so cute!"* type of love that we all encounter during these fresh faced years of high school. I truly love him. This dark, moody boy. He is not the same as anyone else. I told you, he is beautiful. But not just his looks. From his personality, to his sharp features I have memorized in detail, he is just, well, beautiful.

The next question is, of course, does he know? Does he feel the same way? Well, I do not know the answer to either of those questions. Byron has the ability to look at me and know how I am feeling (yes, I also wear my emotions on my face), but he is as as transparent as pea soup. So, I suppose there is no uncomplicated way to answer those questions, but I can try.

Does he know? Maybe he does, maybe he doesn't. He must see it on my face, and know that I care for him more deeply than anyone. Yet, he has never approached me on the subject, because that is just not how he is. Byron is a thinker, he contemplates the world before he speaks only a few words.

Does he feel the same way? Ummm, once again, maybe? I am not a good judge of the whole feelings thing. I know more about this boy than most, but not enough to quite understand his thought process. I hope he feels the same way, he allows me to bombard him with my presence and our bond is obvious to everyone, so I know he loves me. But, does he love me, the way that I love him? Up until now, I'd say it is doubtful, but I will wait. Just being near him, well, in a way, that is good enough for me.

"Ella. Ellaaa. ELLA." Wait, what? Oh. Class. My eyes drift back to reality, and I smile at Mr. Dwayne so he knows that I am sorry.

"Sorry, Mr. Dwayne, what section would you like me to read?" I can tell he contemplates not telling me, but he enjoys hearing my read aloud. His features relax and he smiles,

"Glad to see you joined our planet again Ella, start reading from the top of page 59."

Chapter 2

"Man, Ella, always spacing out in class." Emily jokes with me after class.

"Yeah, I know, I can't help it, always in my own little land." I laugh, knowing my friends are always getting annoyed at my tendency to stay quiet for hours while they all jabber away about the latest gossip.

"Yes, your own little land. Ella Land, that is what we shall call it. Haha, yes, Ella Land." She laughs at her own joke, and I know that Tara and Samantha will soon be joining in on my "Ella Land".

"Ella Land? I like it." I smile at my own thoughts once more, "Well, I am going to head to my study hour, I will catch up with you later." I try to escape, but she is adamant on our in between classes conversation.

"El, study hour? Can't you skip out just once? Wait, you don't have to answer that. I already know what your answer is. See you after, nerd!" Emily sashays away, still chuckling at her own humor. Probably happy that she has finally named my space out sessions, Ella Land.

I love that girl, but she doesn't understand my need for my own time. Not many of my friends do, only Byron. He needs his time alone as well, another thing that I love about him. We can sit in silence for hours, and that would be okay.

I also need to keep my GPA up if I want to be valedictorian this year. I have not gotten all A's since the beginning of junior high just to have it all fall apart my senior year of high school. I have been waiting for that day. When my grades and abilities will put me above the rest. Plus, I am hoping for scholarships to the college that I want to attend.

Aah, study hour. Time to space out, and do what I need to. No more thinking about the frivolous everyday activities, or love pains that I am forced to endure. It is now time to educate myself. Time to dive into the world of math and science. I check the clock, and quickly make my way to my locker to grab what I need before I hit the library. My favorite time of the day.

"El?" I look up to encounter Byron giving me that quizzical, yet humorous look he does.

"Oh hey, what are you doing here?" I fumble around, trying to cover up the obvious doodles on my Calculus homework. I may have taken a break from the brain numbing work my study hour calls for.

"Haha, I was going to ask you the same thing, but then I realized it is your study period. Well... from the looks of it, you seem to have gone a bit astray from the whole study part." He laughs at me, nodding at my artwork. "You know, you are really good at drawing, you should really take it more seriously. I mean, as in, not drawing it on your homework. I feel like that is the only time I ever see it."

"Whatever, I know you are just mocking me!" I glare at him, as he continues to laugh at me. Although, I know he is right, but I don't tell him about my sketchbooks in my room filled with my drawings or the endless amount of notebooks I have filled up with words. That world is mine alone.

"Would you like some help?" He asks, then quickly backtracks knowing I hate it when he offers, especially twice in one day, "I mean, would you like some company while you're doing homework?"

I can't help but lessen my glare and allow him to take the seat next to me, knowing my study hour would be ruined, but in a way that I didn't mind at all. As he settles into the seat next to me, I can smell the musky scent of his clothes and the fruity shampoo he uses. He immediately dives into his backpack, setting up his area, getting into "the zone," as I call it. I let him begin working on the same homework as me, not asking him any questions (and knowing better), him not offering any answers until I am unable to do it on my own.

I finally break, "Okay, how do you do this one?"

He looks up, with that same shine in his eyes, "Oh, that one? Here, let me explain, then we will work it out." He knows how my brain works, I have the tendency to interrupt the explanation before he is done, but he is patient, and allows me to figure it out on my own.

The remaining time passes quickly, Byron helping me as I work out the ridiculous problems of this disastrous subject. Soon, the bell rings, letting us know it is time for next period.

"Looks like we have most of it done, I guess we will be able to goof off in most of Spanish today."

"Yeah, and we won't get yelled at for having our math book out again." We laugh. Our Spanish instructor really dislikes the fact that we understand the language enough to study other subjects during her course. But, hey, I get Spanish, not Calculus.

"See you in Spanish, Ella," Byron says, already walking away, probably to find his friends for lunch. I try not to let my eyes follow him as he goes, I need head to my locker before my friends and I ditch out for lunch at one of our houses. Wonderful perk of living in a small town where your house is only a couple minutes away.

The rest of the day goes quickly by, and before I am prepared, it is time for the game. The game that I have been mentally preparing for all day, we have got this. This is the time where my shyness and insecurities run away, I am a part of a team. I am already riled up before our coach sits us down for his pregame speech like normal.

"You ready for the game tonight ladies?! Time to get pumped up!" Coach Briggs yells at us as he continuously lifts his arms; his attempt at pumping us up. The whole scene is usually more humorous than stirring, with his bald head glistening and his fat rolls animating with his movements, but we have learned not to laugh.

I decide to give in to the poor man, considering I am the captain. Yes, I know, I try to overachieve in as much as possible. "Lets go ladies! We have got this tonight, time to get your head in the GAME!" I offer, with Tara, Samantha, and Emily backing me up.

"We have got this, let's do it!"

The uproar begins, as we huddle up in the locker room, preparing ourselves for the game. Coach Briggs tirelessly going over the plays we have been practicing since the start of the season. This game is the game that will decide if we make it to Regionals or not. Everything we have been working towards, counts tonight. They are not only our rivals, but the obstacle standing in our way to victory.

We make our way to the court, resting on the sideline, waiting for the music to begin before we make our way to the net. I am at the front of the warm up line, the ball in my hands, my friends behind me with the rest of our team. The music starts up, it's time to go.

I begin dribbling the ball, making my way around the court, with my teammates close behind me, pumping up the crowd. I look into the crowd, eyes searching, I see my parents, my friends…. And, the boys' team, waiting to play after we have finished. My eyes continue until I see Byron and we make eye contact. He smiles at me, and flashes me a thumbs up. He has faith in me! We can do this! My heart does flips. My adrenaline is flowing through my veins, this is what I play for, let the game begin.

"Oh my gosh, I am soooo tired!" I proclaim, as I slump into my seat next to Samantha on the bus. Homeward bound at last. Every muscle aches, I can always say I gave it my all after games like this. It was worth it because we won.

"I knooooow! What a game though right?" Samantha asks.

"Yes, it was quite a game, but I am ready to head home." I am not much of a talker after a competition, no matter what it be or how well we did. It is as if my brain just shuts down, and only wants to relax for the remaining hours of the day.

"Oooh, El, please don't tell me you are going to go home on a FRIDAY night after we just won one of the biggest games of the season?" Oh, Friday. I seem to have forgotten.

"Umm, no?" I chuckle, looking sheepish towards my party obsessed friend. They will want me to go out, they always want me to go out. Sometimes I enjoy it, and other times I don't, I am still deciding on what one it will most likely be tonight if I agree to go.

"Come on, Colin's parents are going out of town, and you know everyone will be there."

"Well, it won't be everyone if I don't go, now will it? Besides, everyone? All 60 members of our class you mean?" I reply sarcastically, referencing the small size of our school. "I mean, it isn't like I grew up with them or anything. Oh wait…" I snap my fingers and laugh.

"Stop being such a buzzkill! You know you will have fun once you get there, I will make sure of it."

"Is it back in that field again? He doesn't even have them in a house, but a shed! How cliche can Marcellus be?" Good ole Marcellus, I can't wait to get out of this town someday. I mean, I love it, but well, you will see what I mean.

"Shut up, haha. You are going, call your parents, you can stay at my house tonight." Samantha shoves her cell phone in my direction.

"I will call them on mine, so pushy! Are Emily and Tara going?"

"Is that a real question?"

"Yeah, is that a real question?!" Emily and Tara stick their heads over the seat behind us, putting in their two cents and letting us know they have been listening the entire conversation. Waiting, I am assuming, to see if Samantha could (as usual) talk me out of my hermit shell for the weekend. I am lucky that my friends have known me since we first started school, or Byron might be my only friend.

"Haha, I guess not, okay, hold on. Be quiet, I will let my parents know." I reach for my cell phone, grinning at my friends. I do love them, and maybe I will have fun. *"Ring…ring…ring…"* Man, they better answer, my parents are terrible with their phones. I mean, what if I really needed to get ahold of them? *Hello! You have reached Sarah and Kevin Cane, please leave a message after the beep!"*

"Hey mom! I am staying at Samantha's tonight. Love you! See you tomorrow!" I click my phone shut, and smile at my friends. "Who is ready to paaaartaaaay?" I wiggle my butt in the seat pretending to dance, getting a laugh from Samantha in return.

"Yay! I heard there was a keg too, I bet all the boy's team will be there also, we can celebrate our victories together!" Tara giggles, "And maybe, Nate will be there." Here it comes, the real reason we all go out. Boys.

"Or Ryan!" Emily chimes in.

"Or Matt, or Scott, or Butch!" Samantha explodes, as we all start laughing. "What???" She asks, bewildered. Samantha has always been a fan of the boys, more is always better. I know that I am expected to name someone, so I throw out the name I always do, the boy who I have been crushing on since second grade, before Byron came into my life.

"Oh nothing, haha." I chuckled. "Maybe, Zachary will be there." There, I said it. I am a teenager, I am still allowed to have crushes, not just burning loves.

"What is this? Am I hearing something about a boy from you?" Emily squeals, and squeezes my leg. "I am sure he will be there. I mean, he plays on the basketball team with Byron." She winks at me, still assuming she knows things that she just as well may, I mean I already told you, I never have been good at hiding things. Especially with someone I have known my entire life. I may not have told her about my "true feelings" for Byron, but she knows that I act differently around him than my other guy friends. I am just not ready to form those words just yet, to anyone! I can hardly even understand it to myself. Besides, I am still a 17 year old girl, and boys are boys.

"Ha, Byron rarely goes to those things, but I can probably ask him about Zachary!" I chuckle. Zachary is one crush that I can confide to my friends about. They need something to gossip with me about, don't they? I mean, I can't really explain the deep connection that I feel with Byron with them, they just wouldn't understand. They would giggle at me, and proclaim that they knew it all along, then continue to pester me about telling him my feelings. Yet, they would not understand how I felt because how can you know that kind of love, when you have never felt it yourself?

Don't get me wrong, I know that my friends mean well, and they would embrace anything that I chose, but they would not really get it. They would laugh, like it was simply a crush; a case of friends falling for each other. Nothing is ever concrete in high school, things come and go with the passing fad. This is not a passing fad, I would be devastated if I ever lost the connection that he and I have. Our friendship means more to me than frivolous, fleeting crushes.

But, that is how they would see it. As a minor teenage crush. High school puppy love. If he rejected me, life would certainly move on in everyone else's world, but mine. So, you see, Zachary is safe. He is safe to gossip about, to crush on, to have these "goo goo eyes" that I have for him. The connection is not as deep as Byron; only skin deep; barely grazing the surface.

Zachary is the quarterback of the football team, the lead scorer on the basketball team, the state champion in track. He is nerdy. The type of attractive that most girls have yet to realize is attractive. I captured his attention with my opinionated views on the world, my love of anime and independent films, my passion for sports. We have clicked on most every viewpoint that matters to the teenage soul. I like him. And, I hope I see him tonight. I really do.

"Well, whose house are we getting ready at?!" Emily jolts me from my thoughts, bringing me back to the events of the evening.

"Mine! Definitely mine! I even have some sexy clothes that we can convince Ella to wear." Samantha winks at me, "For her lover boy!" We all break into girlish laughter, my deep thoughts cast to the side for the remainder of the busride.

Chapter 3

"El, you can't possibly be thinking of wearing your hair like that?" Tara tuts at me. I look into the mirror at my hair, still in a ponytail from the game.

"Umm, I think the right answer for this is a no?" She gives me that exasperated look. "No, my final answer is no." I put my hands in the air as surrender and she snaps my hair from the rubberband. I wince and she laughs,

"Good answer. Sam, come do El's hair."

"Geeeeez El, can you do nothing for yourself?" Samantha chuckles at me, and comes over to do my hair. As soon as she approaches, my nose wrinkles, she reeks of Victoria's Secret perfume, and she looks like a 21 year old with the amount of makeup she has layered on. It actually looks good on her though. My friends always have the ability to pull off these outrageous outfits they wear. I look into the mirror again, at my messy flop of faded blondish brown hair growing out at the roots.

"Ooh honey, are you sure you want to wear that?" Emily looks down at me, while Samantha picks up my hair and begins combing the knots out of my sweaty hair, leftover from the game. She makes a face as she eyes my roots, and I give her a dirty look, daring her to remark on my hair. She ignores me and keeps combing.

"Okay, now what is wrong with my outfit?!" I whine, looking down at my hoodie and jeans. The perfect outfit for a cool Fall night hanging out at a bonfire in the boondocks.

"El, you always wear that. Well, or one of your other weird outfits. I know you are all about being you, and blah blah blah, but, don't you want Zachary to notice you?" I turn my scowl to Emily, and check out what my gorgeous

14

friends are all wearing. Perfect hair, the perfect makeup, dark skintight jeans, and sweaters that are less sweater, more tight tank top fabric. To me? They look like they are going to be cold. Oh, did I forget to mention adorable flats on all of them? Do they really expect those shoes to not get muddy? I am a realist, I do not want to ruin things, I prefer comfort.

"You guys look like you are going to be cold. I mean, you look gorgeous, buuuut, I would rather be warm. And comfortable. It isn't like they don't see me everyday at school anyways!" I have a point, not that it really matters, I won't win this fight.

"Haha, oh Ellie, I love you!" Emily jeers at me, reverting to my childhood nickname that I still have yet to outgrow.

"Okay, done!" Samantha smooths a bit of my combed out hair, "You look good Ella, don't let Emily make you feel bad. Zachary already likes you, and everyone knows you are a badass, so who cares?" Samantha finishes my now (in record time) straightened hair, and steps back to admire her work.

"Awesome, are we ready now?" I ask, resisting the temptation to put my hair back into a ponytail. I can feel Samantha's eyes on me as I play with the tie around my wrist.

"First, give me that hair tie." I sadly relinquish the band to her. "Now, we are ready. Let's go! Tara, you driving?" She asks as she puts my hair tie around her wrist. Emily gives me a 'you shouldn't have messed with it in front of her' look of sympathy.

"Noooo way, I drove last time!" Tara whines at us.

"Ugh, fiiiine. But, I am not parking my car anywhere near the party. One dent on it, and I am DEAD." Samantha retorts, wanting to go to the party and not argue about driving.

"Deal! Lets go!" Emily shouts, and races to the car, probably for shotgun.

"SHOTGUN!" Tara screeches, knowing that Emily is running towards it and will not give it up once she is in it. I hang back with Sam, and listen to her lie to her parents about where we are going. Once we get in the car, we turn the music up and drive.

The ride there is filled with loud music, bumping and screaming our little lungs out to the latest Miley Cyrus and LMFAO. My worries, and hermit like behavior, all forgotten once I am with my wild group of females. I love these girls, and my hair really does look great. I am so excited for the night to begin. Isn't this what it is all about? The carefree life of the American, small town teenager. I feel alive, I am excited! The night is young and so am I! I wonder if Byron will be there?

"Well hey there ladies!" Colin greets us as we walk into the light provided by the bonfire.

"Hey, is this where the party is at?!" Samantha flirtatiously smiles at Colin, her previous boys forgotten. Colin is the captain of the soccer team, and his blonde hair and blue eyes match Samantha's. She has always had a weakness for him, she just hasn't admitted it yet.

"Haha, I think it is. Congrats on the win by the way, and Ella, great three pointer man. Sick shot." He looks at me, cheesy smile on his face. Oh, how I love the people I have grown up with.

"Aww, thanks man! I was pretty nervous. It was a close one."

"Well, you pulled it off! Now, are you ladies ready to party? Let me escort you to the keg." He slides his arm over the giggling Samantha, and leads us over.

"There she goes again. How does she mesmerize those guys like that?" Emily leans over to whisper to Tara and I, Samantha already too far ahead with Colin to hear.

"Heck if I know, I stumbled over my feet whenever I get approached." Tara sighs at us, and I nod my head in agreement. I can only seem to talk with boys if they are just my friends, anything else, and my tongue is tied.

As we get to the keg area, the party seems to be hopping. Everyone from our grade is here, as well as many of the under classmen females. Typical. How our grade loves the easy freshman. "Do you see all these underclassmen? What skanks." Tara launches into her hate of freshman rant, where I decide to zone out and scan the surroundings. She can hate the underclassmen all she wants, but we all know each other, so what is the point really.

Everyone must have came after the game. Our small town loves to cel-ebrate, hick style. How many people can say that their idea of a good time resides in a field around a bonfire with a shed (a nice one at least) for the colder season parties? Pick-up trucks and tractors all around. It is almost beautiful in its own way. I bet the city folk who listen to country have no idea how true its stereotype of the country tends to be.

"El, are you zoning out AGAIN? How many times in one day? Here, grab a cup, lets go play some beer pong!" Emily shoves a beer into my hand and drags me over to the beer pong area. In case anyone is unfamiliar with "beer pong". It is a game played on a long piece of plywood with cups on either side. The teams stand on either end of the board, shooting ping pong balls at the other team's plastic cups (normally red cups, ever heard the song red solo cup? Yep, that is where it comes from).

"Haha, I wasn't zoning! I was checking out the area! Okay, let's play! Where did Tara go?" I look around for her, but she has wandered off, leaving Emily and I together, like usual.

"Oh, she wandered off somewhere. You know our friends, ha. Now, who is up next?!" Emily looks at some guys from our grade playing. She always can take the words right out of my mouth.

"Well, it was supposed to be those ladies over there. But, I think I know you don't really care who is up next, do you Emily?" One of the guys, Nate, laughs, knowing full well that the ladies he was referring to were freshman and Emily was not having any of that. Because, in a small town where everyone knows everyone, there is social ladder, and the freshman have to work for it. Especially, when my grade bands together. Emily makes her way to the table, and I follow behind her, waiting for the uproar from the girls we skipped over.

"Waaaait, we were up next!" One of the girls cries, making the wrong move of defying the upper classmen. She must not know the guidelines yet, poor thing. She is a smaller girl, with dark, straight brown hair and big mousy brown eyes.

"Excuse me? Who are you?" Emily snides, and before the girl has time to reply, Tara walks up. Which, in this case may be a bad thing, because you see. Tara is the princess of the school, sidekick to Samantha. The perfect body, rich parents, and an attitude like no other. With Samantha, they rule the school. I just got lucky to know them when we were all learning our ABC's.

"It doesn't matter who you are, we are next!" Tara smiles cheerily at the girls, and they know who she is. They may have an attitude against Tara's friends, but never Tara. I guess it can kind of be depicted as mean girls, but we aren't really that bad, we have the same cliques as every other high school.

"Oh, sorry. We can go after, my name is Rebecca and this is my friend Maggie. I absolutely love your hair." The mousy girl, Rebecca retreats back to the bonfire, dragging her friend, Maggie with her.

"See, no problem!" Tara laughs, throwing her hair back and looking over at Nate. I think she may be showing off a bit, looks like he likes it though. Nate is a wrestler, so he is shorter but muscular. He has shaggy brown hair and blue eyes, but his smile is the best. It goes well with his easy going, cocky attitude, just Tara's type.

"You are such a bully Tara, haha." Nate slides his arm over her, confident that he will get what he wants. "Now, how about you be on my team?" He teases.

"Oh, Nate. You sure know how to flatter a girl. I would love to! Us vs. you guys!" Tara cheers, as we envelope the table.

As soon as I am about to agree to the teams, I look across the lawn and see Byron. Byron with his friends, Jerry and Rick. Those three seem to be inseparable, always goofing off and making funny videos. This party did not seem to be their scene, well, at least not Byron's. I have seen Jerry and Rick at parties before, but rarely can they drag him with them to these things.

Jerry had vibrant red hair with freckles spotting his face, while Rick has dark black hair and dark skin. Their features collide so drastically, it makes their unlikely duo even funnier. They are much more outgoing than Byron at social events, but they are the type that stay was from sports. They have been friends with Byron for as long as I have.

As I am about to head over in their direction, Emily grabs my arm to begin the game. "Ella, let's play! You can say 'Hi' to him later."

"Okay, fiiiine. I just wasn't expecting him to actually be here. I called him earlier, and he gave me the typical not my scene kinda thing. You know, his good kid crap." I laugh, thinking of him drinking, or even smoking a joint. The two most popular choices in our school, the drinkers and the stoners. Me? Well, lets just say, I am not as good of a kid as a lot of other straight-A athletes.

"Ha, well let's play? I am sure he will come over sooner or later." Emily winks at me, and chuckles under her breath. "Or," she says, "Someone else may come over first!" She throws her head to the right, and I see Zachary heading over in our direction. It's my turn to shoot, I am horrible at this game. Basketball has no influence here. I miss. "Dangit, I hate this game. I am just so bad at it! I am going to make poor Emily lose!"

"Ooh, you are not that bad El, just need a few more drinks in yah!" Tara yells at me from across the table, preoccupied with Nate.

"Yeah, I am sure you will make the next shot Miss Basketball." Zachary joins the conversation, smacking me on the shoulder. I almost shudder, getting goosebumps from his touch. Further proof of my aloofness.

Emily shoots me a sidelong glance, reading my uncomfortable composure to the touch. I brush it off. I am a teenage girl, I have got to get over this. I mean, I have never even had a boyfriend. Dates? Kind of. But I am more of the have a crush from afar type. I think for my senior year of highschool, it is time to get a bit more out of my box. I angle my body towards him.

"What are you willing to bet on that?" I ask, giving him my best smile.

"Oh, we are betting now are we?"

"Yep! Sure are, or are you too chicken to wager a bet?"

"Smack talking now! Okay, I will go grab your next beer if you make it. But, if you don't, you owe me a date." He drops the ball, this is what happens when you flirt? I might pass out.

"Oooooooooh!!! Ellie, you blushing down there?" Nate chides at me, making Tara giggle in the process. I am blushing, and his comment yelled over the table makes me blush even more.

"Psh, no. Game on." I reply. He is flirting with me, like usual. No wonder I get those butterflies whenever he talks to me, he is just so adorable. Look at those eyes, man... Concentrate, I close my eyes and pretend I am shooting a free throw, I shoot the ball, and score!

"Ha, go get me a beer, Beer Bitch." I laugh, nudging his shoulder so he knows that I am joking. Everyone laughs as he walks away to grab me another drink. I can do this, I am enjoying this, even aliens could see my smile beaming right now.

"Now, wasn't that interesting." Emily smiles at me, "I am glad you are enjoying yourself Ella, it is about time you stopped all that waiting around for Byron and realize that Zachary is madly in love with you." Then she laughs as she sees my deadpan facial expression, knowing she had gone too far, "I am just kidding Ella, love you." She hugs me, her breath already reeking of alcohol. She must have had more drinks than I thought. I see the water bottle in her pocket. Vodka, more than likely. I grab it.

"Now what is this Em?? Holding out on us? Haha" I take off the cap and chug a bit, yep, vodka. It burns as it descends down my throat.

"Haha, you know me, don't you my love?" She grabs the bottle back, and turns to shoot the ball. I begin jeering at her, until I feel a tap on my back.

"Finally get my beer, Bitch?" I ask, turning around expecting Zachary with my drink, only to see Byron, looking quite surprised at being called a beer bitch. I want to take back the words immediately.

"Beer Bitch, huh? Sounds like you are having fun like usual Ella." He gives me that look, the same one I see from my parents. Disapproving, but happy that I am being a teenager, the kind of look most have trouble deciphering.

"Oh, sorry! Buzzkill! What's up? I didn't expect to see you here, getting your drink on?"

"Ha, you know me, but actually, I am drinking tonight." He lifts up his beer so that I can see.

"Really? What made you decide to let loose a little bit?"

"I don't know, just thought it was about time to start living it up!" He raises his beer higher into the air in mock toast.

"Excuse me, is this the same Byron I know?" I ask him, raising my beer into the air as well to cheers him.

"Oh be quiet Ella," he laughs. "I just thought I would come say hi, but it is your turn, so I will talk to you in a bit. Don't slur your words too much tonight." He chuckles again at me, and turns to walk away, bumping into Zachary as he turns.

"Oh sorry Byron, just bringing Ella some drink."

"You mean being the Beer Bitch? Haha, I am kidding. It is cool. Have fun." He eyes me warily, and gives a head nod to Zachary, walking back towards his little group. I can't help but keep my gaze fixed on his retreating form, my best friend is drinking? How odd… And the way he was acting? Even more suspicious, I make a mental note to check on him later.

"Here you go. Hopefully I didn't spike it." Zachary playfully winks at me, handing me the red cup. I snap back into the moment, and lift my head to meet his stare.

"Ha, hopefully you did." I giggle, forgetting the oddity of Byron's look and the drink in his hand. Everyone deserves to let loose a little bit, even the boy whose lectures still haunt me on my party habits. I throw back the beer, and miss another shot.

"Ermahgersh, what a party right?" Emily slurs at me, as she begins walking towards the direction of the keg, forgetting we are in the middle of the beer pong challenge.

"Oh yeah, it is great. Umm, Em? Beer pong?" I reply, trying to hand her the ball, but she ignores me.

"Sooo, Zac was ALL OVER YOU. Maybe you should go see what he is up to." I am about to tell her to be quiet because he is still here, but I turn to see she is right, he has already walked off elsewhere, my moment gone. I sigh, and laugh at my drunken friend, although I can feel my blood beginning to warm.

"Ha, are you trying to hook me up Miss hasn't even talked to Ryan yet? Oh look, he is right over there. Why don't you go say hi?" I spot Ryan on our path. He is taller and tends to wear only athletic gear, but he is sweet. I decide on a plan, I grab Emily's vodka bottle and take another shot, prepping myself.

"Naaaah, you know me, I like to admire from afar." Once again, taking my thoughts to make them her own.

"Shut up, don't worry, I have got a plan." I wink at her.

"What is your…." Before she can even finish her question, I push her into Ryan as he walks past our table.

"Woah Emily, way to be clumsy!" I laugh. Her face red with embarrassment, she glares at me, but I can see her lips trying not to twitch into a smile.

"Well, hey Emily, I was hoping to see you around here. Are you okay? Bit tipsy?" Ryan teases her, his eyes lighting up. Everyone can see that Ryan absolutely adores her, except for her. Typical. Even with my incessant nagging at her, that he likes her as well, and she should stop avoiding him whenever possible. Sometimes, you just have to take charge for yourself, for the greater good.

"Oh no, just a bit clumsy! And, well, maybe a little tipsy." She giggles and I see this as my cue to leave. She doesn't even notice me as I slip into the darkness, away from the unfinished game. Now, where is everyone else? Tara and Nate seem to have also disappeared, this could be a good sign, I hope she knows what she is doing. Where is Samantha? I turn my head to the largest group of people, she seems to be the center of attention more often than not. Yep, there she is, with Colin still on her arm. I do not know how she does it. She is just magic with the boys. Actually, I do get it, she is just so charismatic. I begin to walk over to her, before I see Byron.

He is still standing with Jerry and Rick, along with a group of kids that graduated last year. I wonder what they are doing? I think about heading over there, but I would rather not. Byron tends to like his space, and I doubt he will want me cramping his "style" as he jokes with me about. Sometimes, we are seen so often together that people assume we are something more, which is of course, inaccurate.

And, I do not want Zachary getting the wrong idea, especially since my best friend has never given me any sort of attention like that. You know, the kind that warrants that there may be something more. I am deciding on which group to head over to when my decision is made for me.

And, as if reading my thoughts, there he is. "Hey there Ella, whatcha doing standing over here by yourself?" Zachary saddles on over to me from the group that Samantha was in.

"Oh you know me, just standing back and watching the party."

He laughs, "is that so?"

"No, I was actually just headed towards Sam, just looking around to see who else is here." I can feel the effects of the shot loosening my tongue.

"I see, where is your partner in crime?"

"Emily? She just happened to trip in the right direction." I smirk, jerking my head towards Ryan and Emily still talking by the fire.

"I think I get it. About time she talks to him, he has been trying to talk to her for a while now. She sure knows how to play hard to get!" He laughs.

"Right? It is like the whole school can see it except for her." I laugh at the silliness of it all. Even Zachary knows about Ryan, I hope that something sparks between them tonight. Emily has never been good at choosing boys, but, I like Ryan. He is a nice guy.

"Yes, it is like the whole school can see it except for her…" Zachary stops, and looks at me.

Wait, is he leaning towards me? I close my eyes, just as his lips touch mine. I can smell the alcohol on his breath, but then again, it is on mine as well. Otherwise, I do not think I would have had the courage to kiss him back, especially with Byron so close by… Byron? Why am I thinking about my best friend right now? No, just no. This is my moment. My moment with this boy who wants to kiss me. This boy who wants to be with me. This is what I need.

I wrap my hands around his neck and kiss him back, forgetting the party going on around me.

Chapter 4

"Gaah, my head feels like it has rocks in it…" Sam moans from beside me, sprawled out next to me on her bed.

"Tell me about it!" Emily whines from the floor, "At least you guys passed out in a bed."

"STOP YELLING!" Tara cries from my other side, throwing her pillow at Emily's head.

"I wasn't yelling! You just yelled!" Emily cries, throwing the pillow back, missing, only to hit me in the face.

"Oh come on guys, go back to sleep. What time is it?" I check the clock next to the three of us. "9:30? For real??" I am too tired and hungover for this. I slam my face back into the pillow. Maybe, if I just go back to sleep, they will leave me alone. Why must they wake up so early on a Saturday? We literally wake up early 5 days a week, sometimes more! I am not what you would call a morning person.

"Awww, forgot that Ellie hates waking up early!" Emily taunts at me.

"Well, that is just too darn bad!" Sam rolls over on top of me, officially ruining anymore sleep I thought I could get. "Wakey, wakey, eggs and bakey." As she continues to lay on me, until I groan and throw her off onto Tara, officially starting the wake up war. The pillows begin whacking me in the head, and I grab mine too slamming it into their sides. Aah, yes, you are thinking. The typical girl pillow fight, well, this is not a 1950's ad. You are sadly mistaken. 17 year old girl in 2009? Head bashing, and heathenish cries, while we are all still in the wrinkled clothes from the night before, bags under our eyes, streaked with traces of last night's make-up.

"Okay, okay truce!" Samantha howls, "We are going to wake up my parents, and I really do not want to explain to them why we were out so late last night." Even though Sam may have the coolest parents, they still would not approve of a party going into the early morning. I wonder what lie she told them that they actually believed?

"Oh you would pull that card you pansy." Emily jeers, dropping her pillow in defeat.

"Now what? Since I figure none of you are feeling sleepy anymore." I grumble, knowing full well that I would love nothing more than going to bed. My friends may be morning people, but I for one, am not at all as I claimed before.

"How about we grab some food and discuss the night's events?!" Samantha cries, smiling at me mischievously. Oh God, what did she see? How drunk was I towards the end? Oh maaan, Zachary. We kissed, then what? My mind hazily tries to recapture the previous night's escapades. Byron… I think I talked to him after that. Oh man, I do not want to discuss this. What did I say to Byron? My flashback replays vividly in my now sober memory.

"Ella, I like you, and I am not quite sure how you feel about me, but if you kissed me back…" Zachary stares down at me, this cute boy who likes me, and I think I may like him as well. Yet, all I can think about is Byron, I wish he would kiss me like this. Maybe, someday… Why must I think like this? I am too cowardly to tell him my feelings, but I need to, before this. So, I can choose with an open mind. My drunk mind is whirling, I know what to do.

"I like you too Zachary, I think I just need a minute. Okay?" He looks at me quizzically, but he understands, in a small school like this, it is hard not to know someone. To know how they may react to things, I like that. He smiles at me after a minute.

"Okay, I know you are drunk, haha. I will be over by the fire, I am all ears when you are ready. Oh, and call me Zac." He leans down and lightly kisses me again, then turns around and walks back to the rest of our friends. I smile, Zac, I like that better.

I know what I should do, I need to go find Byron. He should be easy to spot, I turn around to hunt him down, and there I see him. Standing by the trees with Jerry and Rick, his eyes glued to me. Was he watching? He smiles at me sadly, and I beckon him over. I see him say something to Jerry and Rick, it makes them laugh, and they grin at me. How is Byron the only one blind to my affections?

"What's up Ella." he asks as he reaches me. He reeks of marijuana. Weed? Since when has he ever approved of smoking? "Are you smoking weed, Byron?" I look at him incredulously.

"So what if I am? I can try new things too." He snubbly retorts. Well, obviously he hasn't smoked that much, still Byron. Now or never. I ignore the nagging in the back of my inebriated brain than Byron is acting weird, I need to tell him how I feel. Is this a good idea? Who cares!

"Byron, I want to talk to you..." I whine at him, did that come out as a whine?

"Ella, you are drunk, what do you need? Are you okay? Should I take you home? I saw you kiss Zac, are you okay?" He is genuinely concerned for me, as usual. The amount of sober rides this poor kid has had to give me are endless. And, we have only been able to drive for about two years now. Sigh.

"No Byron, about us." He is so unobserving sometimes.

"What? You are one of my best friends, you know that Ella." He knows where this is going, his face tenses up, prepared, but not for what my drunk ass of a self states.

"Byron, I love you."

"Yeah? I love you too, Ella." He laughs at me, "You really are drunk." He doesn't believe me, he never takes me seriously. I am suddenly angry.

"NO BYRON, I am in love with you. Can't you see that?" That stuns him, he just stares at me. Speechless. I have made this boy speechless, great. "Say something..." I whimper. My confidence sliding away as I understand what is going to happen. He continues to stare at me, until he finally sighs.

"Ella, you know I love you. But, it has never been like that. You are my best friend, I could never lose you. And, I am not in my right state of mind right now, trust me, we are better off friends." An excuse, just like I knew would happen.

"I hate being friends, I want something more." I embrace him, hugging him, crying into his chest. He wraps his arms around me, "I know Ella, I have always known. But, maybe someday, you know both are brothers think we are going to get married. I just can't bring forth those kinds of feelings for you right now." I begin crying, drunk and embarrassed, crying in the arms of my best friend who just turned me down, as I knew he would. "Oh Ella, you drunk mess, I am sorry. Someday you will understand...." *His eyes glaze off, as if in another world. What does my best friend think of?*

"I am sorry Byron, can we forget this?" *I do not want to talk about this anymore, I want it to go away. Blame it on the alcohol. Ha.*

"Of course Ella, you are still my friend, as you always will be." *I wipe my nose on my sleeve, sniffling once more.* "Now, can we please go get a drink?" *I laugh, he always knows how to ease my aching, even if it is over him.*

"Okay, lets go you heartbreaker." *I slug him on the shoulder, heading back over to the keg. The thoughts already erased, is that a tear I see him wipe away?*

"ELLA, oh my gosh, I knew it!" Sam snickers at me, whacking me me once again, with a pillow.

"Whaaaat?" I laugh, shaking my head at the painful memory. How could I be so stupid as to go off spouting my eternal love for someone right after he saw my kissing someone else?! And, the fact that I knew I should not have done it, this is why I can't drink.

"What do you mean what?! You and Zachary! I totally saw you guys getting all smoochy in the dark, don't you dare lie!" Samantha jeers at me, the accusation stunning Emily and Tara into fits of giggles. Zac. Oh my gosh, I forgot all about Zac.

"Hahaha, you kissed Zachary?!" Emily giggles at me, making kissy faces with Tara. I blush. I had so much to drink that I forgot anyone could have seen. Oh, the teenage angst.

"He prefers Zac and okay I may have kissed him..." I laugh, hiding anything else I may have felt. I can admit to some things, just not what is too personal even for me to recall.

"Aaah!!!" The cheering commences, it looks like I will have a lot of explaining to do. I shake Byron from my thoughts, and allow my friends to fill me in on their adventures of the night.

Monday has come too fast. I am choosing to drive today from my house, instead of the usual walk from my grandparents. I want to avoid everyone at all costs. Even if that means taking my menace little brother Reese, to school. Luckily he is always too tired to talk most mornings, so my drive to school allows me to think.

What am I going to say to Zac? To Byron? Damnit drunk Ella, why weren't you thinking? Those teenage hormones too much for you? Gosh, how can I face them? Byron's locker is right next to mine. Sigh. Let the week begin, at least I have a couple of tests to think on and practice to take my mind off of it.

I put my van (yes, my mom's minivan) into park, and let Reese out while I sit thinking, not wanting to go in. Reese mumbles something unintelligible at me, before wandering off zombie like to find his other sophomore friends. I guess it is now, or never. Hopefully I can make it to my first class without bumping into anyone at all. I speed walk towards the school, and make it to my locker unnoticed, maybe this will be easier than I thought.

"Hey Ella…" I whip around, face to face with Zac. Could this day start off any worse? Damnit. I let my guard down. I calm myself inside my head. I have got this, I like him, I will fix this.

"Hey Zac, I am so sorry about the other night…"

"It is okay, you were pretty drunk, haha." He is laughing it off, this cute boy who would wait for me, even if I was too drunk to make a decision. I know my decision now, I don't know why I was worried.

"No, it isn't okay, and I am really sorry. I was an asshole, but I want you to know that, I like you too, Zac." I stand up on my tip-toes, wrapping my arms around him, and I kiss him. Just like that, in the middle of the crowded hallway next to my locker. I mean, how many times in life do you get to be a teenager with not a worry in the world. He kisses me back before the cat calls from the hall start. I pull away smiling. "I would like to try this, if you would." I blush, looking down at my shoes. This is new for me. Especially personal displays of affection, but hey, you have got to start somewhere.

"Ha, I would like that too, El." He smiles from ear to ear, it begins. "Well, I have better get to my first class before I get reamed. Not all of us are perfect students." His teasing is back, the awkwardness erased.

"I saw that El!!!!" Emily sneaks up behind me, grabbing me from behind to pick me up and spin me around. "Hahaha, you are so cute!" She continues to squeal, "I mean, perfect match. The studious, nerdy, athletic perfect match up! You guys can talk anime, then go for a run."

"Oh stop it, don't make this so huge, haha." Even though I am smiling.

"But it is, when is the last time I could convince you to tear your gaze from Byron? Hmm?"

"Be quiet, haha." My mood begins to lighten, someone wants me back. A simple kid likes me for me, no quiet brooding or times when I know I should not talk. I am happy, ecstatic really. Byron is my best friend, he will always be there, and I am ready to move on. It is time to stop worrying about everyone else and enjoy my last year in highschool, with a boy! I can't help but smile again.

"Let's go to class before we are late, Emily." I put my arm around her and begin walking towards our class.

"Psh, you know that Mr. Dwayne loves you, he will yell at everyone but you! His little track star." She punches me in the arm, I wince, and laugh. She is right.

"Okay, okay, let's go." I pick up my pace, and she starts talking about Ryan with that dreamy look in her eyes.

Out of the corner of my eye, I see Byron, leaning up against a locker, looking rather downcast. Nothing will ruin my mood, but I head over there anyway. Emily knows what I am doing and rolls her eyes at me, breaking from her daydreaming.

"Actually hang on, I will meet up with you in class." She waves me off, dismissing me, and I make a beeline for him. Might as well face him too while my adrenaline is already pumping.

"Hey, put a smile on buddy!" I give him my biggest cheesing it smile. He chuckles, shutting his planner that he must have been writing in, as usual.

"Sometimes, you can't fix sadness Ella." He looks right at me, I stare back quizzically.

What does he mean by that? His mood is so much different than at the party. His mood swings are getting too much for me to handle, if only he would ever just talk about his problems instead of being so cryptic. I brush off my annoyance, wanting to cheer him up anyway.

"Of course you can, you are young! You want to talk about it?" I ask, knowing his answer before he says it.

"No." He finalizes the conversation, walking away from me to his class. I am left standing in his spot, as the late bell tells me that I am going to get a lecture from Mr. Dwayne.

What did Byron mean by that? What is eating at him? What an odd thing to say, even for him. Perhaps, I should just put it out of my mind. This week has been a happy blur (aside from the harassment of my friends on Zac, and Byron's strange comment).

My life has been rather blissful for the past few days. We won our two games this week, as well as the boys winning theirs. I haven't really talked much with Byron, but Zac and I are officially a couple. Which happens rather quickly in high school. You just kind of decide to be together and that you are off limits to others. That is what it seems to mean to me. Besides the typical hand holding and note passing, we aren't too affectionate with each other. I suppose after being friends for so long, that is a hard thing to adjust to. For some… I reign my thoughts in from straying.

"Hey Ellie, what are your plans this weekend?" Emily rams my shoulder with her own, catching me as I am closing my locker to head home for the weekend.

"Hmm, not sure, maybe going to see a movie with Zac. Our first real date, ha. How about you?" I play if off casually, not wanting her to know how nervous I really am.

"No clue, since there is no game tonight, I am at a loss!"

"Maybe you and Ryan should double date with us!" I joke, knowing full well she would not ask him such a thing.

"Well, actually… He did ask me on a date!" She was almost bursting to tell me, I laugh at her enthusiasm.

"Really? Oh my gosh, I am so excited, what are you guys going to do?"

"I don't know, he said he will call me when he gets home." She blushes, looking down at her shoes. Typical Em.

"Let me know how it goes. My brother is probably waiting in the car by now, so call me when you get home from your date!"

"Of course, later Ella!"

I grab my backpack, and make my way to the van. I usually just have my dad drop me off at my grandparents, then I walk to school but occasionally I feel like driving. I just avoid it because Reese is constantly having me take him everywhere.

We get along well enough for teenage siblings, but he is not patient when I choose to take my time after school. I guess that goes for me as well, I have left him a couple of times when he took too long. At least, he is the only one I have to worry about. My two older brothers are out of school.

"Way to take forever El!" He whines at me, already waiting by the van. His light golden hair flopping in his eyes, and his green eyes dark against the pale sky. He got my mom's side of the family, looking nothing like me and being a foot taller.

"Oh be quiet, like you haven't made me wait."

"Yeah, but you just leave me."

"You are fine, You can always walk to Grandpa's. Besides, it isn't like John didn't used to leave me." Stating a fact, my elder brother was in the same predicament as me, a senior when I was a sophomore. Poor Reese does not know that I have waited for him much longer than John ever did for me.

"Okay, fine, will you take me to Eric's? I am going to stay the night there."

"Sure, have you asked mom?" He never asks our parents anything.

"Nope, you want to tell her?" Called it.

"Reese, come on, you have got to start asking her, instead of leaving me to get bitched at."

"Okay, next time, I swear! So, yes?"

"Yeah, last time though." Normally, I would just take the little twerp home since I had warned him, but I did not want him at the house when I got there to call Zac about our date. He tends to get on the other line, and listen in. Oh the perks of being the only girl.

"Really? Cool! I would ask why you are so cheery, but I don't really care that much."

"Fair enough." We ride in silence with the music blaring the rest of the ride to his little friend's house.

I don't really mind our silent car rides, it gives us both time to unwind from the day and be in our own thoughts for a minute. The fact that we are in each other's presence can be comforting, when it isn't overwhelming. I already know the way to Eric's house, I have dropped him off there numerous times. I almost know all of his friends' addresses by now, I could crash any party I wanted. But, who really wants to go to an underclassmen bash? Not me.

Luckily, the house is only a couple minutes from the school. I pull into the drive. "Okay, have fun. Call mom later." I warn at him before he jumps out of the truck, grunting, and grabbing his bag to walk away.

"Bye!" I cry after him, as he gives me a backwards wave, someday he will appreciate me a little more. I just have to give it some time, highschool isn't really the best for siblings so close in age to cohabitate peacefully anyways, too many hormones going crazy.

I shake my head, smiling, and backing out of the drive. Now, time to plan my first date. I drive quickly down the backroads to my house, Eric's house being 25 minutes out of the way. I get in the house and the voicemail is already blinking. It's Zac, he will be here in an hour. Why did that kid have to live so far away? An hour?! That barely gives me any time.

What should I wear? I have never been on a real date before. We decided on something simple- Dinner and a movie. Should I dress casual? Chic? Sporty? I feel like I have an outfit for everything but a date! What have I been thinking, not getting date clothes? I guess I have not thought about this as much as I should have. He will be here at any moment. I wish I could call my friends, but I know they have already left their houses for the night or never even went home. I'm desperate and call my last resort. I pick up the phone and dial the number I know by heart.

"Hello?"

"Hello, Mrs. Rood, this is Ella, is Byron home?" I can almost hear her tone change through the phone, knowing it is me.

"Oh yes, sigh, let me go get him." I am not sure if she really likes me. She acts like I am a burden when I am over at times. Perhaps, I am. I do show up

randomly most of the time without a forwarding notice, but it is so easy because Byron is normally home. Also, he lives right down the road from my grandparents, so it is easy to go there when I am bored and stuck in town. I am his rival for most awards and recognitions at school, and I often take him away from his studies. Oh well! She loves my older brother, John who is best friends with Byron's brother. (Ironic small town stuff I know) So maybe I will wear on her.

"Hey Ella, what do you need?"

"Hey, I have got a question for you, and all my female friends are out. What do you think I should wear on a date?" I hear him shift the phone to his shoulder and audibly sigh. I can picture him shaking his head at me.

Silence.

"Hello, Byron?" And, then I hear a chuckle. I relax, we are still okay.

"Hahaha, oh Ella, I love you. I am presuming this is with Zac?" I can hear the smile in his voice. He thinks I am funny. I should have known that our friendship could never be tampered with. My wonderful Byron. How I love him.

"Yessss."

"Haha, I bet you are blushing right now. I pay attention Ella! Hmmm, you really want my advice on this?

"Sure do!" I laugh at his energy, he must be in a good mood for once.

"Well, I think that you should wear some nice jeans and a nice top. Whatever feels good to you. Whatever you are comfortable in. You are beautiful no matter what you wear, Ella..."

Did he just call me beautiful? He did... I giggle. I wish he meant it in a different way.

"Thanks buddy. I think I know what to wear now. You are the best." I smile into the phone.

"Don't you worry Ella, have a good time. Call me tomorrow and tell me how it went, okay?"

"Sure thing..." I heard a knock on the door downstairs. Oh no! Looks like my dad will be the one to answer the door. "Well, I think he is here, bye Byron!"

"See you later, Ella." *Click*

He always hangs up so abruptly. Having gotten this far, it shouldn't surprise you, he is not one for phones. I know it bothers him when I call all the time, but other times I think he likes it. I smile once again, and grab my bag. I guess I will just wear what I am wearing now- jeans and my favorite shirt. Sometimes, Byron really can help. My confidence has soared.

"Ella! A boy is here for you and he says his name is Zachary." My dad booms up the stairs at me, in hopes of scaring Zac I assume. He is so silly, my father. He might be a little frightening as well, considering I have only brought friends over before this. His small frame is still muscular from his daily workouts, and his ashy brown hair is cut short, making his blue eyes piercing. Time to see how it goes.

"Funny dad! I told you about Zac." I canter down the stairs and round the corner crashing into my father. "Ouch!" I whine, rubbing my nose that was scrunched onto my father's chest.

"Woah there Ellie Princess! No need to trample me. I was being nice." My father is holding a Budweiser and smiling from ear to ear, with a mischievous twinkle in his eye. Something was definitely up. I look around my father's bulky figure to see Zac chuckling at me from his seat by the counter.

"I was just giving him a fatherly speech, no need to panic." Dad winks at me and grabs Zac by the neck, "I mean, I have got to rough up the football star don't I? That was one hell of a season my boy!" Zac smiles.

"Thank you sir. I am sorry it is over."

"Oh, at least you are a basketball stud too. Looks like my princess knows to pick them!"

"Your princess, huh?" Zac smiles at me.

I know that I will be mocked for that later. There is no age limit to being called "Princess" by my dad. He will be calling me that when I am 30. It doesn't matter who is around or who isn't. I stopped being embarrassed by it a while ago. It has grown on me, maybe when I meet Zac's parents, I will get some dirt on him as well.

I give Zac a sympathetic look for dealing with my dad, and try to hurry the awkward transaction that was happening.

"Yep, his princess. Are you ready?" I grab Zac's arm, dragging him towards the door, away from my father.

"Already? He just got here! Your mom isn't even home yet." My dad whines at me, holding that gleam in his eye. He knows I want out of here. My mom would be much more merciful than him, but I was ready to go, he could meet her later.

"Oh, sorry dad! Don't want to miss the movie, it is starting shortly." I give him the perfect excuse. He has no way to hold me here now. I have won this battle.

"Okay, okay fine. Here is $20. Spoil my princess." He chided, as he hands Zac the money and winks at him. Hey, at least we get a good date out of this. My dad can be pretty cool, in his own way.

"Oh, I can't accept this sir." Zac thrusts the money back at my father, just as I intercept it. Grabbing it from his hand. I am not giving back a week's allowance!

"But, I can!" I wink at my father and wave to him as I trot out the door. I hear his laugh and mumble, "Smart Ass!" Before the door shuts behind us.

"Haha! That was fun." Zac hugs me. "The chariot awaits Madam." He opens the door as I climb in, giggling.

"Why thank you, good Sir." My little fairy tale is about to begin.

"So does Applebee's sound good to you?" Zac looks at me from his side view as he drives. Naming the restaurant that is in the next town over in which every high school couple goes to.

"I love Applebee's! Sounds good to me." I smile awkwardly at him as he shifts gear and I hear the engine sputter. I hope this car doesn't break down on my first date. The sound doesn't seem to bother him. Maybe he is used to it.

"Okay, it is settled then… Princess!" He bursts out at me, laughing at his own joke.

"You must think that you are so funny, but I am used to my friends mocking me about it by now, so joke is on you." I cross my arms, triumphant. He throws one hand into the air in surrender.

"Okay, okay. I understand, my mom calls me 'meatball'."

"Meatball?" I laugh. I can't help it.

"Yes M'am. We are Italian. I used to love meatballs as a kid and my dad always said my head kind of looked like one. So, it stuck. I think your nickname is much better than mine." He chuckles, lost in his younger memories.

"I think you are right, Meatball." I nudge him in the arm, as he nudges me back.

We are flirting and my stomach could not have more butterflies in it. Just as I am about to bug him more about his life, he reaches over and grabs my hand. It stops me instantly. His hand is sweaty, like he is nervous. Good, mine must be also. I hear the car grind once more, and I can't help but ask if we are safe.

"Of course it is safe! This baby has a couple of noises every now and then, but I assure you, she is very loyal." He lets go of my hand, pats the dashboard, and gives me a thumbs up.

"Okay, fine. I believe you!" I reach over, and grab his hand once more. He smiles at me, and rubs my thumb. I never want this to end, but I see Applebee's appearing in the distance. He squeezes my hand a moment and then reaches to shift.

"At least we made it here." I joke at him as he pulls into the parking lot.

"Man, your jokes are just as bad as mine, Ella." His eyes are sparkling at me as he tells me to wait a moment, and he gets out to open my door for me.

"Oh, such a gentleman." I joke, but my smile tells him that I am thrilled.

"Anime has great moral lessons for gentleman." He winks at me, it is a known thing that I watch anime. I have no shame, and he is right, it does have great lessons. I want to ask him what shows he watches, but my mouth is too dry from my nerves.

I am so glad that I went with Byron's advice, and wore comfortable clothing. My nervous sweat would be drenching me otherwise. Byron. Why must I always think of him? I wonder what he is doing right now. He sounded so happy on the phone. He must have plans for the night. I will ask him about it tomorrow when I call to tell him about my date. There I go again. I will not ruin my first real date thinking about the many sides of my best friend.

Zac grabs my sweaty hand once more and we walk into the restaurant together, I ban Byron from my brain.

"Table for two." Zac says, and we are instantly escorted to our table, even with it being busy, there are still a couple open tables. I look around for anyone I know, but doesn't look like I will see anyone tonight.

"Doesn't look like anyone we know is here tonight." Zac says, reading my mind, as the hostess tells us that our server will be here in a moment.

"Nope, and that suits me just fine."

"Me too." His lopsided grin tells me that he isn't lying. I blush.

"Hello, welcome to Applebee's, my name is Mona. Can I start you off with anything to drink?" An older waitress with too much makeup on, greets us non enthusiastically.

We both order water, and already know what we want. I order the chicken basket, and he orders a burger along with cheese sticks for an appetizer.

"Cheese sticks, great choice! They are my favorite." I admit to him.

"Mine too, how can you go wrong with fried cheese?"

"I know right?" And, the conversation has started. It is so easy to talk with Zac, not at all what I was expecting from a first date.

We begin talking about everything under the sun from our similar interests like anime to our individual interests, mine being writing and his love for card games, and soon we start talking about sports.

Our appetizer arrives shortly, and the cheese talk starts once more, I am surprised I have not done anything embarrassing yet! As we continue talking throughout dinner, not a single one of my thoughts stray to anyone other than Zachary. He is wonderful! Our conversations not halting nor or any silences feeling uncomfortable.

"You want to run track in college? That sounds like so much fun!"

"Yeah, I do. I know it is a lot of work, but I think I can do it." He says, the passion he feels showing in his face, making him so much more attractive to me.

"I think you can too." I smile back at him.

"Okay, okay, real question."

"Shoot!" I almost yell, putting another chicken piece into my mouth.

"Will you go to prom with me?" My jaw drops; food almost making its way back onto my plate, but I hold it in. Prom is months away. MONTHS. This is entirely too unexpected. He sees a future with me? It has been a mere week, I do not know what to say. My mind is reeling, I cannot be rushed into things like this. I need to figure out something to say before my word vomit is expelled.

"Zac... Prom is so far away, can I say probably?" Too late, my thoughts came too late. His expression cannot be unseen, I have hurt him. Again. Already. This isn't my fault, couldn't he ask me to the winter formal first instead? Like normal people?

"Oh well, I am sorry. I just figured that I have liked you for so long, and I just thought that... Nevermind, I understand Ellie. I know that I will persuade you soon, here's to the evening!"

The worry on his face is wiped away as I smile back at him, and reply, "I know you will. How about asking me to the winter formal first?" Batting my eyelashes at him, trying to erase the awkwardness that ensued his comment.

"That would have made more sense." He sniggers at himself. "Yes, will you go to the winter formal with me first?"

"Of course, I will Meatball." I use the nickname I so recently discovered.

"I will take it! To winter formal!" He lifts his water glass to cheers, and I wave my chicken finger at him, chuckling all the while. Soon the awkwardness passes, and we are both in fits of laughter.

We finish our dinner with the banter of a new couple getting to know each other for the first time. Zac pays, and we make our way to the theatre.

The theatre is packed on Friday night, of course. I see people I know from school this time, we smile and wave, still lost in each other, not caring about who we see anymore. I insist on paying for the tickets, much to his dismay, he did pay for dinner.

"My dad gave us $20, let me use it!" I beg him, using my puppy eyes that never fail.

"Fine, but I am getting the popcorn and drinks." He pouts back at me, showing off his dimples.

"You bought dinner, it is my turn." I continue to argue.

"No way, I will let you get the tickets, that is it. What kind of pop do you want?"

"Mountain Dew.... Extra butter on the popcorn too!" I laugh, giving up as he walks towards the concession stand, on a mission. I can't stop smiling, even as the man at the counter waits patiently for me to declare which movie I will be seeing.

"Two for Harry Potter, please." He tears the tickets, grabbing my money.

"$10.50, it will be in theatre three on your left."

"Thanks." I take the tickets, heading for Zac, already waiting at the end of the concession stand. I have been wanting to see the newest Harry Potter for a while now, I have read all of the books, so has Zac. This is the sixth movie, sixth book. I have officially grown up with Harry Potter, reading the books as they were released, and the movies soon after. Not many kids in my school still enjoy the fantasy series, claiming to have grown out of it. I am glad that Zac has the same taste as me, I would hate to have had to drag Emily here. She thinks it is too nerdy.

I choose the seats, choosing the middle area perfect for my viewing pleasure. He takes the seat next to me, just in time for previews, one of my favorites things about attending the movies. It takes you to another land even before the picture has started. I love the escape. Zac casually takes my hand in his, like it is the most normal thing in the world, the lights begin to dim, just in time.

"Man, Harry Potter is one of the few movies that actually do the books justice." I claim as we are driving back home. The movie was great, he didn't even try to make out with me though, I can admit that I am little bummed. I was hoping for my first movie theatre make out session, but we were both too into the movie.

"I agree, loved it! Don't you wish that life was like that sometimes?"

"What? Full of war and power struggles; it is." I tease him.

"You know what I mean, with magic. Another world, one different than this one. Wouldn't that be amazing if there were something more?"

"Yes, I think that would be grand." I look at him, he is lost in his thoughts. Probably playing quidditch in his head, I giggle. Life would be so different if magic were possible, what if life were like the movies? I would prefer my life to be more of a comedy than a tragedy. The type of movie with an epic ending of happiness and success. I weigh the options of saying this out loud, deciding for it.

"I would prefer my life to be a comedy, yah know? Life has too many tragedies in it for me. If I could choose, I would create for myself the perfect happy ending."

"Hmm, I see what you are saying. So philosophical, Ella. Mine would be a comedy too, so I guess I could not be Harry Potter because his life is nothing but a tragedy!"

"Yeah, no way would I want to be him. Imagine losing all of your loved ones."

"Not all, he keeps his two best friends. Sometimes, that is all you need."

"Haha, yeah I guess you are right."

Before I realize it, we are pulling into my driveway. He puts the car into park, and positions his body towards me. "I had a great time tonight, Ella. I hope you did also."

"Of course, I did. I had a phenomenal time!" I grab his hand, and gently caress it with my thumb. His skin is coarse, that of an athlete. He looks at me, relief flooding his features, "I am glad. We better get you inside before your dad threatens me again."

"My dad threatened you?! I knew he was up to something, why didn't you tell me?" Panic rising in my voice, my dad can be so obnoxious.

"Haha, I am just joking Ellie! Let me walk you to the door." He kisses my cheek, and gets out to open my door. The perfect gentleman, I punch him on the arm to let him know that his joke was not at all humorous. Before, I can take my hand back from the punch, he wraps his arms around me and leans me slightly onto the car. We fall into each other, his lips find mine, and this time, my thoughts are not jumbled from inebriation. My thoughts are on the way his lips taste like butter mixed with salt, and how soft they are.

After a couple of minutes, he withdraws from me, and kisses my nose. "Better get you inside, Ellie." He whispers in my ear, I do not want to go inside. I want to stay right here, but my logic tells me otherwise. My parents will be up waiting for me. Their precious only daughter, out on her first date. "You are right, I will see you Monday?"

"How about I call you tomorrow?"

"That sounds good to me." I wave him away, as he heads back to his drivers door, his gaze lingering on me. "See yah later, Zac."

"Later, Ellie." He never used to call me Ellie, but right now, he can call me whatever he wants. I am smitten; something has changed. He is winning my heart out from another, slowly but surely. I smile to myself and head inside, preparing myself for the bombardment of questions from my mom.

Chapter 5

*T*he weeks have been speeding on by, studying and practicing for the Final Tournament takes up most of my time, along with my friends too. Zac and I still find time to see each other, but I have not seen much of Byron lately, he has not been in school as much and he has missed my Friday morning breakfasts that I make with my grandpa every week, he must be sick. I make a mental note to call him soon if I do not see him in class today.

The winter dance is almost here though. A chance to dress up, and relax for the night. Zac and I will be going together, he should have just asked me to this one before the promposal, but by now, I will say yes to anything he asks. We have been dating for over a month now. A whole month. An eternity in the eyes of a teenager. I think I am in love with him, but this time it feels different. I know I will word vomit it eventually.

"Hey Ella, you ready for the dance?" Emily pounces on me mid thought, with Samantha and Tara on her heels. The whole gang already crowded around my locker before the day has even begun. It seems to be the only time we all get a chance to catch up.

"I sure am, how about you guys?" I smile, knowing that they will all have dates by now.

"Well, Sammie is going with Colin, and Tara is going with Nate!" Emily squeals, and Samantha cuts her off.

"Yeah, and Emily forgot to mention she is going with Ryan!"

"Oh, my little Em is growing up!" I grab her in a bear hug, she shoves me off, laughing.

"Yeah, yeah, I figured since my best friend could grow some balls to get a guy, so could I."

"Oh, I am sure that is what you were thinking." I laugh, smacking her on the shoulder. Our relationship can be so aggressive.

"Also, I invited Zac to breakfast at my grandpa's tomorrow morning."

The last few weeks had gone by in such a wave of new activities, I had almost forgotten about my morning breakfasts with my grandfather. I always remember them last minute, calling him to make sure he has the ingredients for our morning bake off. Then, I hurriedly call my friends to let them know that breakfast is still on. Byron was the only one who never needed reminding, but lately he seems to have been in a daze also. I must remember to ask him about it when I call him. I think back to last week's breakfast, what had we even had? My mind has been scattered since I had begun dating Zac.

"Oh, inviting the boyfriend to breakfast, huh?" Tara croons at me, "That must be a big deal since our breakfast club rarely changes!"

"Yes, right? I figured I may as well invite him, since he keeps distracting me from it anyways!" I giggle, flushing at the thought of our make-out sessions in his car before I head to my grandpa's for the night.

"Oh my gosh, TMI!" My friends seem to scream in unison.

"Shut up, like I have not heard it from all of you at one point!" I point my accusing finger in their direction, "So deal!"

"Fair enough, it is about time you gave up on Byron and actually looked happy anyways." Emily states matter of factly. My face flushes, and then drains. Byron.

"I am over this conversation."

"I am sorry, you know I was just kidding. How is he doing anyways? I haven't really seen you two butting heads like usual." Emily changes the subject, knowing my limitations, and I laugh at her reference to our constant bickering. "You are one of the only people who can get such a rise out of that kid, I swear. He seems kind of mopey lately, have you noticed?"

I guiltily reply, "Yeah, I haven't really talked to him too much since I have been dating Zac. I mean at breakfast, and stuff, but I haven't seen him as much. Do you think I should hang out with him?" I haven't even bugged him for study time like usual. Maybe he needs a good girl talk. I feel so badly that I have not even noticed his mood, taking it for his dazing or being sick. Even my friends had taken notice, I must be a horrible friend. My happiness already vanishing as I worry about my friend.

"Yes, I think you should. What if he thinks you are ditching him now that you have a boyfriend?"

"She is right, you shouldn't ditch your guy friends just because you have a boyfriend now." Samantha nods her head, agreeing with Emily and Tara.

"You are right, I will see what he is up to after school today. I am staying at my grandpa's tonight, so I can just see if I can hang out at his house. I haven't been doing that like usual. I have been with Zac." I feel so guilty for ditching Byron all the time and not noticing how mopey he had been. What a terrible friend, I need to find him.

"Okay, well class is about to start, see you guys at practice?" I say, and they nod at me, already onto a new subject while I am still thinking about my best friend. I will go find him at lunch, I start walking towards English, we have a test today, so I actually have to pay attention.

"Hey Byron! Hold up!" I find him at lunch, heading out to eat elsewhere I would assume. At least I caught him before he left. "Where are you headed for lunch?"

"Hey Ella, just going to go home to grab a sandwich." He stops a minute to talk with me.

"Care if I join?"

"Sure, come on." He barely looks at me, what is up with this kid? My beautiful best friend, his eyes look so sad, the twinkle has begun to fade. I follow him to his car and climb into the beat up white car, a Nissan maybe? I don't know, I am terrible with vehicles. He starts the car, and the music begins to blare.

"What is this band? I really like it." Byron is singing along to the lyrics, the twinkle in his eye lighting up once more. Music is magic to him. It has been since I have known him. His emotions so easily lifted or deflated by his choice of music. This band is upbeat, light, and cheerful.

Byron hands me his Ipod without skipping a beat, "Owl City, I like them." I scan the songs from this artist, I will have to look into this band. The drive to his house is short, he only drives his car in the winter when it is too cold to walk. His house only blocks from the school, and only houses away from my grandpa's house.

We arrive at his house, his parents both gone at work. This is my time to question him, he has barely reached his front door before I bombard him.

"Byron, are you okay? I know I haven't been that good of a friend to you lately because I have been so preoccupied, but I want you to know that if you want to talk, you know that I will always be here." I continue my rant into his kitchen while he looks through the cupboards for food. Without turning to look at me, he replies, "Calm down, Ella. I am fine, just thinking about graduating and everything." He eats pieces of the sandwich he is making while making it.

He takes a bite into his already almost finished sandwich, and faces me leaning against the counter. "Why are you so worried about me?" His gaze connects with mine. Why do I worry about him so much? He isn't my responsibility. He has friends other than me, I stop to think about it before answering him.

"I don't know, I guess you just look kind of sad lately, and you are missing school. I wanted to make sure everything was okay." I shrug, trying to act like it isn't a big deal.

"Well, I am fine. I have just been busy with my own thoughts, nothing to worry about." His look betrays him, something is wrong, I just know it. I know his and our boundaries though, we will not discuss it further today. I try to stand by our boundaries after our awkward talk at the party, not wanting to lose his friendship.

"Okay, want to make me a sandwich too?" My stomach gurgles a moment later, and Byron laughs at me.

"Yeah, I can make you a sandwich. PB&J okay?" He is smiling at me, trying to show me that I am worrying over nothing. I want to believe him, even though my gut tells me otherwise.

"Yes, please!" I smile back. I watch him make me a sandwich, and hand it to me, I bite into it as he goes to make himself another one. We spend the rest of lunch joking about the upcoming dance, and eating the entire loaf of bread.

"So, you plan on asking anyone to the dance?" I question, "Maybe that cute sophomore who always follows you around?" I have seen her following him around like a puppy, sitting in his vicinity at lunch, making googoo eyes at him, trying to make him laugh.

"Haha, someone jealous? Nah, I don't think that I am going to go."

"Psh, me jealous? Nah, I know I have your heart." I wink at him, as he rolls his eyes at me, and I continue, "And, what do you mean you are not going? It is our senior year Byron! You have to go! We only have a couple more months together…" He notices my obvious whining, and contemplates arguing with me, but knows he will lose this battle.

"Okay, I might go. How is that?"

"I will take it! Where do you plan on going to college by the way? I haven't really decided yet. I am just so torn!"

"Ummm, I don't know, I haven't looked into it." He hasn't looked into it? That is not what I expected from this control oriented individual. He is looking at everything but my eyes, I want to probe him more.

"What do you mean you haven't thought about it? You of all people! You could get in anywhere!" I blurt out, my word vomit once again.

"Ella, I don't want to talk about it. I just don't know what I want to do with my life yet, okay? Can we drop it for now?" He pleads with me.

"Okay, okay, fine. But, this conversation is not over. We better head out before we are late for Spanish. I know how much you love Spanish!" I make a wisecrack at him, he hates Spanish. I think he spends the majority of it writing in his planner and sleeping. He smiles at me, and his eyes drift into his own world for a minute before he speaks again.

"Let's go Ellie Belly." He uses my old nickname we had as kids, back when I was a little chunky. He is the only one allowed to call me that, besides Tara, who used to use it constantly. I chuckle at him, and follow him to the car. He sure knows how to win me over.

"You ready for breakfast tomorrow? You want to hang out tonight after practice?" I ask him before I forget.

"Yeah sure, what do you want to do?"

"Maybe you can help me with my math, then go shoot some hoops?"

"Sounds good to me." We reach the school just in time for the final bell announcing that lunch is over. I tell Byron I will call him, and race to my locker to grab my things for the next class.

"Hey Ella, you ready for breakfast tomorrow?" Zac meets me at my locker after school, he takes my books from me as I open my locker. What a gentleman. "I sure am, are you ready to wake up that early?" I nudge his shoulder with my own, and laugh at his eagerness.

"Waking up early isn't nothing! It is better than the early morning practice sessions that coach insists we have."

"Oh my gosh, that is so true. I hate it when we have those."

"So, what time should I be there?"

"Around 7 am is the usual." I smile up at him, he is so cute. I am excited for him to come to breakfast.

"Awesome, I think I can do that. What are your plans for this afternoon? Since, I live in town and you are staying at your grandpa's ya know..." Oh, I had almost forgotten that Zac lives in town as well. He lives even closer to the school than Byron, and it is a good thing too because I still do not trust his car.

"I have got plans with Byron. He is going to help me with my math and then we are going to shoot some hoops. You are welcome to join!" I add in, even though I am not sure I want my two seperate worlds to collide just yet. I see the hesitation in Zac, is he jealous?

"Maybe I will, I can always learn some shooting from him. I am going to pass on the math though, you guys are way too advanced for me." He jokes with me. Zac is intelligent, but he is not in AP math like Byron and I.

"Okay, that sounds good, I will call you. Want to walk me to my van?"

"But, of course." I grab my backpack from my locker, and head to my beat up, old van. Of course, my little brother is waiting by the door with his friends. He spots me instantly and they all turn their heads. His little band of boys is what I call them. I know them all by now; Eric, Drake, and Mike. A bunch of knuckleheads, but growing up with them, I love them like my little brothers.

"Awww, Ella and her boyfriend!" Reese whistles at me, and his friends laugh. Zac gets close enough, and greets them.

"Hey there Reese, what's up?" He knows my little brother, and they are on good terms, I think Reese looks up to him because his attitude always changes as soon as he sees him.

"Hey Zac, I still don't know what you are doing with my sister." He jokes.

"Because she is amazing, of course." I giggle, and Zac chuckles back at me.

"You are such a sweet talker," I reply. He winks at me, and my brother's friends all begin to catcall us. "Okay guys beat it! Let's go Reese, I will take you home."

"Actually, I am headed to Eric's with everyone. I even let mom know. I figured I would tell you so you wouldn't be waiting for me. I mean, if you actually decided to wait for once." He punches me in the shoulder.

"Great, see ya later turd. And see yah turd's friends!" I shout at them as they begin making their way towards Drake's car, the only one of them with a vehicle. I turn back to Zac, "I will call you later?"

"Of course." He kisses me quickly on the lips, and heads towards his vehicle. Life is perfect. Time to head to Byron's. I wonder if he needs a ride. I look around for him, nowhere in sight, he must have already headed home. He did have his car today, duh, I should have known that. I will stop by the gas station to get some snacks while we study.

After 20 minutes of scoping out the best candy and pop, I am finally at Byron's. It looks like his parents are here, great. I knock on the door, hoping he would answer, but his mom comes to the door instead.

"Hey Ella, you here for Byron?"

"Yeah, we have a study date. Is he here yet?"

"Yeah, he is downstairs, head on down." She is checking out my outfit for the day, probably not up to her par. She suspects my feelings for Byron and I can assume that she does not find me good enough. My loud, rambunctious personality certainly conflicts with this quiet, thoughtful family. Why does she like my brother, John? He probably behaves himself around the family, but I have never been able to hold in my loudness.

"Hey Byron, way to greet me!" I trample down the stairs and into his room. His room is basically the basement of the house; a little man cave. He is working on a paper at his desk. I come up behind him and tousle his hair, peering at his work. He slams his hand over it, and without turning, says, "Haven't we had the personal business talk, Ella?" He smooths his hair back into place from my ravaging hand. I suppose we have had this talk, the only word I caught was "sadness."

"Yes, I suppose we have. Why are you writing about sadness?" I cheerily ask him.

"Because…"

"Oh come on, just tell me!"

"Because Ella, sometimes you can't fix sadness."

"Oh be quiet with your teenage angst, Byron." I ignore his dreary comment. He must be going through that teenage rebel stage. It was about time he had that stage, I hit it at 15 and quickly grew out of it. I am convinced this is what he is going through, but I am going to cheer him up anyway.

"Oh Ella, haha." He quickly changes the subject, and I bite my tongue from asking him if he is okay again. "Are you ready for some studying?"

"Yeah…. I guess." I didn't really want to, but the homework is due tomorrow and I can't risk getting a B. My college scholarships are depending on it. Byron gets up from his desk to grab his math text, never one to waste time.

The studying goes on for what seems like forever… "Ella, are you even paying attention to what I am saying?" Byron wakes me from my daydreaming of us, crap. By "us" I meant Zac and I… This conflict in my soul is quite troubling sometimes.

"Yeah, yeah. X something and Y something."

"Ella, if you aren't going to pay attention then why do you bother?" He is irritated, with good reason, I space out during his explanations a lot.

"I am sorry, at least this is our last problem! How about we figure it out tomorrow morning at breakfast? I think my brain is about to explode…" He smirks at me, I know I have won, he is getting bored also.

"Fine, ready to shoot some hoops?" He stands up from his cramped position and stretches, cracking his body loudly. I give him my grossed out face, and I get to see his smile again. I live to make this boy smile, I forgot how much I miss him when I don't see him.

"Yep! Is it okay if I invite Zac?" I bounce up, and start putting my stuff into my backpack.

"Of course, I like Zac, he is cool. And, Ella?" He fixes me with his gaze, always one to look right into people's eyes when he wants to say something important.

"Yeah?" I turn toward him him.

"I am glad you are happy." He looks at me with that saddening gaze, and my breath catches.

"Thanks? Okay, Byron, what is wrong?" I am determined this time, I cross my arms and wait for his response.

His face changes, "What do you mean what is wrong? I am fine, I told you that." He glares right back at me, ready to fight.

"You are hiding something from me! What is it?" He stares back, holding my gaze, and then he relaxes. I know I have won this fight already.

"Okay, okay I will tell you. I have been just going through a weird phase, and I have been in a funk. So, I have been hanging out with some new friends. I hope I haven't been neglecting you and I am glad you are happy after our drunken talk that night." He almost mumbles the last part, not wanting to relive our awkward moment when he rejected me.

"Oh, well, thank you, I guess? I knew something was up! What have you and your new friends been doing?" I know that whatever it is, it can't be good.

"Promise not to get pissed?" He asks, running his hand through his hair.

"Of course." What could he really piss me off about? I was just happy he admitted to his funk.

"Well, I needed to blow off some steam, and they have been helping me. You see these shoes?"

"Ummm, yeah? They are nice, new?" I check out his new Adidas sneakers, they must have cost him a lot. Not knowing where this is going, I cock my head, waiting for more.

"Well, I stole them." I gawk at him, he what? What did he just say?

"What do you mean?" I reply softly.

"I walked out of the store with them, I mean Ella, the feeling was exhilarating! My heart was racing, I could feel every atom in my body jumping. I know you don't approve of that kind of stuff, but I just can't explain it." His light is aglow with such ecstasy, I almost don't want to waken him from this sick dream of his. But, I have to, this is not the Byron I know.

"What do you mean you stole them? That is terrible Byron, and so wrong. What the hell were you thinking? You could have gotten caught, or arrested! What is going through your brain? I mean seriously, stealing is wrong, I would never steal in my life. You know how I feel about this. I am so disappointed in you, your new friends must be really messing with you if you think that stealing is okay."

I am furious, I have never scolded Byron like this before, nor have I ever had to. He should know that stealing is not okay, it is wrong. By the end of my rant, I am shaking with anger. I look at him, he has shut himself down once more. I almost regret it, wanting to see him smile again.

"You know what Ella, I knew you wouldn't understand, nevermind. I am leaving, go play basketball with Zac, I don't feel like it anymore." He gets up to leave, and walks out of the basement out the front door before I can react. Damn it! Why does he put me in these situations? He knows that I cannot just condone stealing, and he left me in his house! I get up to race after him and his mom stops me at the door.

"Another fight? Typical." She says to me, I do upset Byron more often than others, but I am sorry.

"I am sorry Mrs. Rood!" I yell at her, and run out after my best friend to fix things.

He is walking at a quick pace away from his house, away from me. I run in front of him and try to block his way, he keeps walking.

"Byron... please stop."

He continues to ignore me, time for drastic measures. I grab onto his front torso and place my feet on his to stop his walking. His steps begin to falter with my weight and his combined, he finally stops, I look up at him. At my beautiful and lost best friend and he is crying. I don't know what to do. I hug his torso harder and place my face against his chest.

"Roody, I am sorry... I didn't mean it, I love you." I use his nickname to soften my apology.

His face is stone, his eyes filled with tears. I haven't seen him cry since middle school when I slapped him for breaking one of my friend's hearts. We look back at this and laugh, but at the time it was quite traumatizing for both of us.

"Roody... I am sorry, please do not be mad at me. You know how I feel about stuff like that." I finally get him to look down at me and can tell he is angry.

I can see it in his features, his flushed cheeks and pursed lips. The looks he gives me is steel.

"Leave me alone Ella."

"No, I won't. Talk to me." My determination has set in, I will not leave my best friend like this.

"I said go away, I am never coming to breakfast again!" He blurts at me. His words sting, he has never threatened to abandon breakfast before. Now, It is my turn to be angry. He has no right to be this angry with me! He was wrong, not me.

"Fine, be like that." I jump from his feet, releasing him, and he continues walking. I let him. He can go pout somewhere else. I head back to my van, fuming, what is Byron thinking? He is so stubborn, but never has he been a thief. I hope this phase of his passes soon. I will not dwell on this. I drive to my grandpa's house.

"Hello?" No answer. Looks like my grandpa is not home from whatever job he is performing today. He may be retired, but that does not stop my grandpa. I drop my stuff off in my room, and pick up the phone, dialing Zac's number. Byron will not ruin my day.

"Hey Zac? Ready for some basketball?"

"Byron not feel like playing basketball?" Zac asks me once we both get to the courts at the school.

"No, he didn't."

I do not feel like talking about our fight with Zac. I do not want people to know that he has been stealing. I also just do not want to talk about the pain that fills my chest when we fight. The hurt I feel when we are on bad terms. I care for Zac so much, but my love for him cannot compare to the feelings I have for my best friend. He is my treasure, and I will mend things between us. Hanging out with him only reminded me of my feelings for him. Maybe I was better off avoiding him...

"That is cool, I like hanging out with just you anyways." He comes towards me with the ball and kisses the tip of my nose.

"Haha, I like hanging out with just you also." I kiss him back, longingly. I may have feelings for two boys, but my hormones sure rage up around Zachary.

Maybe I will lose my virginity to this boy. Oh, did I not mention? Of course I am virgin, I barely have talked to boys besides Byron, and we all know that will never happen. Zac is my perfect distraction; the distraction from school, from sports, from Byron, from my future quickly looming towards me, waiting to engulf me into adulthood.

"Let's play!" I jump away from him, and dribble towards the net for a perfect layup.

"Hey, that doesn't count you cheater!" He jeers and the game begins.

We play multiple games of one-on-one before we both tire, and decide to sit on the bench.

"I think I won." Zac teases me, pinching my side. I smirk at him.

"You only won because I let you, can't let your ego deflate."

"Oh, is that it then?" He jostles me, and the tickle fight begins. Soon we are both on the grass in fits of laughter. He pins my arms down, "I will only let you go if you admit that I won fair and square!"

"Never!" I squeal.

"You are so stubborn, did you know that Ellie?" He looks down at me.

"Yeah, I know." I smile affectionately at him.

"I like it. You are perfect." His lips find mine, and soon we are grinding against each other. He keeps his weight off of me, afraid to crush me, and my hands explore his built chest beneath his shirt.

His hands caress my hips, then he pulls away. "Geez Ella, you are just so beautiful. I think I love you."

He loves me? Do I love him? Maybe... "I love you too." I reply, the second I love you that I have ever spoken.

I do love him, but I am not in love with him. I know that now. His smile lights his whole face. He releases me, letting me up, and we sit on the grass next to each other. We are lucky to live in such a small town that not many pass by the basketball courts. We would have gotten some whistles for sure.

"I have never said I love you to anyone before..." He breaks the silence, showing me a piece of his soul. One that I cannot reciprocate, not honestly, so I tell my first lie.

"I have not either." It is not really a lie, Byron does not count. He is my secret, my best friend, my someday. But, that may be years from now, maybe never. It is no use to tell someone that, especially my kind, loving Zac.

He squeezes my hand, my mind goes to us once more. I cannot let another perfect moment be spoiled by my over thinking. This moment where I told my first boyfriend that I love him, and I do, I do love him. I am so excited for breakfast tomorrow. I wonder if Byron will come?

Chapter 6

"Ella, you are burning the toast!" My grandpa yells at me.

"I am not, and not as bad as you burning the bacon!" I crack back at him, happily. My grandpa lost my grandma five years ago, that is when I started making breakfast with him. I began staying the night once a week at his house, and one day we decided that we should begin making breakfast before school. My parents and brothers came, then Byron joined. Soon I had all of my close friends attending. It was our thing, and we had fun with it. I was sad that this was my last year making breakfast with him, but I told Reese he had to start where I left off. It was agreed upon.

"I do not burn the toast, people like it crispy." My grandpa mumbles at me.

"They like it crispy, not burnt!"

"Oh be quiet!"

"Ella, we all know your grandpa is the real cook here!" My dad butts in and teases me from the table, always the first to arrive. My dad gets to the breakfasts early, so he can make it to work on time, he tends to side with my grandpa on my cooking. They think that they are so funny. I hear the door slam shut, another person is here.

"Woah, look who is here! Why would you invite him Ella, aren't you afraid he will dump you after trying your cooking?" My dad snidely yells at me, at that moment I know it is Zac, I do not even have to turn around.

"Hey Mr. Cane, hey Ella." Zac's eyes find mine, and we share our moment before my grandpa interrupts, "Who is this strapping young fella, Ella?"

"Haha, this is my boyfriend Zac, Zac this is my grandpa." He approaches my grandpa to shake his hand.

"Nice to meet you Sir."

"Well it is nice to meet you too! Grab a plate, breakfast is serve yourself! I would stay away from that toast though, Ella has the tendency to burn it." He winks at Zac, and hands him a plate. My family, a bunch of jokesters.

"I will keep that in mind sir", Zac laughs and begins filling his plate. I am impressed by how he takes it all in stride, his family must be the same way with new people as mine.

After that my father leaves, and everyone else begins trickling in. Emily, Tara, Samantha, my mom, and Reese. Just as breakfast is about over, I hear the door slam once more. Byron is here, I knew he wouldn't miss a breakfast.

"Hey Byron!" Everyone cheers at him, eating their meal. He greets them all warmly, and comes to the kitchen to grab a plate, ignoring me.

"I made your favorite, blueberry pancakes." I put three pancakes on his plate, and smile at him, trying to break the tension.

He smiles at me, "I figured you would." Whenever Byron is mad at me, it is easy to appease him with his favorite breakfast foods. Blueberry pancakes and french toast, he hates eggs, so whenever I make eggs for breakfast I am always sure to make him his own french toast.

"Are you still angry with me?" I ask him, getting right to the point.

"Never one to beat around the bush are you, Ella?" He laughs, "No, I am not. I am sorry I was so rude to you, forgive me?" He puts down his plate, and grabs me in his arms, pulling me in for a tight hug. A hug? Byron never hugs me first, he must really be upset over our fight last night. What a great start to the day.

"Of course I do! We will talk more about it later, okay?" I hug him back, smelling his shampoo, before the day taints the sweet lilac smell.

"Did you just smell me, Ella?" He changes the subject, I chuckle, he would catch me in the act.

"Maybe, I did. Go eat your pancakes." I shove him away as we laugh together.

We are fixed, all is well in the world. I have the best friends that I could ask for, a wonderful boyfriend, and the winter dance is almost here long with winter break! Plus, our last game of the season is tonight, a sad but happy time. If we win this game, we will be Regional champs along with boys who played their last game a week before us. Life is good.

"Ella, are you ever going to eat your own breakfast? We are going to be late, I told Ryan I would hang out with him before class starts!" Emily yells at me from the dining room. I roll my eyes at Byron, and we head out to finish breakfast before the day begins.

"I am never going to get the hang of this stupid math!" I whine at Byron as he helps me finish the last problem we never got to the night before and forgot to do at breakfast. It is study period, and math class is up next after our spanish class, luckily Byron forgave me or I would never get this homework done.

"Ella, you haven't even tried to do it on your own." He is trying to keep a straight face.

"I have to." I huff, crossing my arms and leaning my head back to dangle it behind the chair. "We could just play crossword or something the rest of the period, if you would just give me the answer…"

"Sigh, you know giving you the answer isn't going to help you on the test. I am just trying to help you remain Valedictorian."

"You mean help your nemesis who is challenging your position?" I poke him, and wiggle my tongue at him.

His serious face fails, and he beams at me, "You know there can be two of us, it is called co-valedictorians. I am good at sharing." He chuckles, and nudges me, but not to be coaxed out of the task at hand, "Now, figure it out and don't bother me again until you have at least attempted to finish it."

I grab my pencil in defeat. Fine, I can do this all on my own. I begin solving the difficult problem. My mind reels as I look at Byron's dark hair falling in his eyes as he is hunched over a book. His eyes already long gone into whatever world of his he tends to enter, he never smiles when he gets into his mood. In my Ella Land, I smile all the time, his world must be much darker than mine. I wonder where his thoughts stray?

I finish the problem right before the bell dismissing us to our next class goes off, "Byron, is the answer right? Check it before we go to math!" I frantically cry.

He grabs my paper and nods his head, "Right answer, hopefully you did the work correctly."

I smile at him, "Doesn't matter, I got it right, lets go!" We head to our lockers, Spanish class, then math is up. I can double check my work in Spanish and study for the math test that I am sure our teacher has planned, I think it is some kind of movie day anyway.

Spanish class goes by too quickly, and math is here. I am tired from the movie watching, and from last minute studying. Byron has it so easy, he just sleeps the movie away and will probably still get 100% in the course.

"Ready for the test?" I ask Byron, he shrugs his shoulders and heads to his seat. "I will take that as a yes?" I laugh, then I look at the shirt he has on, I haven't seen it before. "New shirt?" I question him, following him to take my seat in the back acrossed from him.

He looks down, "Oh no, it is my brothers."

"Haha, I see, hope you didn't steal it!" I joke at him, then I see his face, and wish I could take it back. His face is contorted in anger, he did not find my jab at him funny. It is too soon to make a joke about our fight, dangit it Ella, this is when you use your social protocol! The clouds begin to form in his eyes, and I know his moods are getting worse...

Byron gets up from his seat and glares at me, "You know what, sometimes you can be a real bitch." He walks out of the class, everyone gawking at us, unable to speak, Byron never speaks out like that. I want to disappear, I did not think he would react like that...

Emily rolls her eyes at me from her seat on the other side of me, "Wow, did he overreact!" Emily, my only friend in AP math with me, at least I have her.

"Yeah, I think he did..." I mumble at her, sinking lower in my seat. I feel like a bitch, I should not have said that. This is the most fighting we have done in years.

"Don't worry about it El, I am sure he will get over whatever stick is in his ass! You guys will get over this little tiff. Ready for this test?" Emily, always so relaxed, she knows just what to say to take my mind off of something.

"Yeah, I am, I hope Byron gets back to it."

"He won't fail a test just to spite you El, he will probably be back in the next few minutes."

"You are right." And, right she was. Five minutes later, Byron comes back and apologizes to our math teacher. He takes his seat next to me, pointedly ignoring me, and you know what, I can ignore him too. I did not deserve that, I mean I was just kidding, if I am a bitch, then he is a jerk.

Mr. Roberts passes out the test, and the rest of the hour goes by with only the sounds of pencils scratching and my very loud thoughts about my best friend's behavior. He of course, finishes the test in record time and is allowed to leave the rest of class for the library. I want to follow him, but I know I will take until the last 5 minutes of class to finish this test. I retract my thoughts about Byron, and continue with my test, even his teen angst won't ruin my perfect GPA.

"Hey beautiful, ready for your game tonight?" Zac greets me at my locker at the end of the school day. I pry my mind away from how I did on the Calculus test and about Byron. The game, time to concentrate on something else.

"Sure am!" I am excited, last game of the season tonight, unless we some-how miraculously get chosen for the championships after winter break. The championships are a battle of the divisions after the season has ended, only the top teams in the conference get chosen. The boys team did not, so I figured our chances were gone if they could not get chosen either.

"That is the spirit, well I have got to run home and change for your game. I will be there cheering you on!" He quickly kisses me, and whispers, "I love you, you are going to do great." Then he is gone. Even with the oddness of the day, nothing will get in the way of our last game. My last game as a senior, then what?

Life continues, what will I even do with my life? I can't even think about it, I do not want to grow up. I prefer this childhood I have perfected, concentrat-ing on what I am told to. It is a good life, an easy one. I have everything I need, right here.

"Ready for the game?" My friends walk towards me, already in their warm up gear for the game ahead. They all have the blessing of having gym last period, so they are all warmed up.

I chose band instead, the music soothes me. I am a trumpet player, I love it. They usually mock me for forfeiting my ultimate jock status for band nerd instead. I just laugh along with them though, how can I explain to my friends that music gives my mind a rest, it calms my soul. The same goes for my art class, I love drawing and painting, creating whatever is in your head. Allowing it to pour out. My parents want me to go to college for business, but my heart screams for something else. Sometimes, I don't want to hide it.

"I sure am, how about you ladies?" They fall into step beside me as I head to the locker room to change as well.

"I am definitely not, this is so sad, our last game of the season. I might cry." Samantha replies, grieving the loss of her princess of the school status. Tara laughs, "Oh you are just going to miss the power!"

"What?! I am offended, and have no idea what you are talking about!" Sam flips her hair back haughtily, a smug smile on her face. She knows exactly what we are talking about.

"Oh be quiet Tara, you know you are going to miss all the boys fawning over you!" Emily pinches Tara's side, and wags her tongue at her. I laugh, oh my wonderful friends, I am going to miss them when we all leave this place.

"Hey now, nothing wrong with giving the boys a little shake!" Tara retorts.

"Oh nothing at all. But, I think I am going to miss you guys all the most." Emily replies.

"Okay, enough of this sappy crap, game time ladies!" I yell at them, pulling on my sweats from my locker. I am the strong one, I will not wallow in what has not even come to pass yet. And, I really do not like thinking about it.

"She is right!" Coach Briggs yells from the locker room entrance, "Is everyone decent? I need to go over the game!" I look around, all of the girls have their uniforms on, we are ready for the game and I am ready to think about nothing but my pounding heartbeat on the court.

The game was rough, and it was a close one, but we won 53-50, a last minute three pointer by Samantha for the win. We are Regional champs! A beautiful way to end the season, we are all happy.

"I can't believe I made that!" Samantha screeches in the locker room, jumping around like a lunatic. We all high five, taking our seats for the after game speech.

"Great game ladies!" Coach enters, his booming voice riding over the rest of ours. "Spectacular way to end the season! Especially for our seniors." Samantha, Tara, Emily, and I are the only seniors, the remainder of our team is made of juniors. "Now, no sad speech tonight, but we will be having practice at the end of winter break just in case we are chosen for the championships! So no grumbles, I expect to see you all here the second Monday of break, even you Seniors. Next year will be hard without you, but we still need you. Now get dressed, and go celebrate!" We all cheer, the juniors patting us on the back and congratulating Samantha on the last shot to win the game.

The locker room begins to clear out, my friends and teammates all going to greet their families in the gym. I always take the longest, I like taking a shower after the game before I see the faces of the crowd. And, I enjoy reflecting on the game before, but tonight it is different.

This was my last game of my high school career, things are changing. Next year everything will be different, no wonder Byron has been so moody lately, he must be thinking the same thoughts as me. I frown down at my feet, change is hard. With that thought, I grab my bag and head to greet the crowd.

"Good game, Ella." Byron is the first to greet me, waiting outside the locker room, away from the gym. What is he doing here?

"Thanks, Byron." I slide past him, ignoring his obvious position of wanting to talk.

"Wait, Ella, hang on. I am sorry for my outburst today, okay?" He grabs my arm, I yank my arm out.

"Okay, Byron, but what you said was uncalled for. I was just kidding, and that was just mean." I blurt out my feelings of anger and humiliation from our previous encounter.

His face turns red, "I know, I am sorry Ella. You really did have a great game though, I will see you at the dance tomorrow night." He veers away from me, towards his waiting friends waiting for him by the concession stand. Two apologies in one day, I swear he is moodier than usual. I watch him walk away as my parents fast approach me, time to put on my smile.

"Great game Princess, what a way to end the season!" My dad grasps me in a tight hug, and kisses my mouth.

Gosh, he is so embarrassing, "Thanks dad, haha." I wipe his wet kiss from my lips, and turn to my mom's waiting figure. She is still beautiful, even at 50. Her dark brown hair contrasting against her pale skin, her dark brown eyes lighting up when she sees me.

"Great game sweetie!" She hugs me, and hold me for a moment longer. "My little baby is growing up." She kisses my forehead, wiping a tear from her eye. My mother, always the dramatic. I don't mind though, she reminds me to enjoy life.

"Oh mom, you still have Reese, stop it!" I swat her away.

"Yes, I suppose so. John and Luke are all grown up, I never even see Luke anymore… You better go to college nearby!" My mother whimpers at me. It has been a while since Luke has made an appearance at any family function. He is my eldest brother. He moved to California when I was younger, and rarely visits. It is quite traumatizing for my needy mom.

Thankfully before the conversation can go any further, Zac appears beside me.

"Regional champs; victors!" He picks me up, and swings me around. I can't help but laugh, and join his excitement.

"Regional champs! Mom, Dad, is it okay if I hang out with Zac for a minute?"

"Oh yes, we will see you at home sweetie." My mom answers before my Dad can object, and she grabs his arm to steer him away, "No later than 11, Ella!" My Mom reminds me of my curfew.

"Yes, I know. See you guys!" I turn to Zac, and latch my arms around him, hugging him tightly. "I am so happy we won!"

"You guys did great, great season." He agrees, holding me in return. I nuzzle my head into his chest, he smells like cologne and laundry soap. I take this moment in, my moment.

"Thanks, you guys did too." I smile up at him.

"You ready for the winter formal tomorrow night?" He asks me.

"Sure am, I hope your tie matches my dress."

"I doubt it, I am terrible with matching colors."

"Of course you are."

"Now, what is that supposed to mean?" He backs up from me, still smiling.

"Oh, you know. You are a boy. Boys are terrible with that kind of stuff!"

He laughs at me, "I guess you are right. Well, even if we don't match perfectly, it will stay be a great night. I promise."

"Okay, I believe you. We are still meeting at my house right?" I ask him.

"Yes mam! My mom is out of town, so she won't be home."

"Won't be home, huh?"

"Haha, she will be back by tonight. She knows teenagers."

"Well, damnit!" I joke with him, we have discussed sex, but never really planned on it. Joking about it makes it easier to talk about.

"I know, don't worry, I can still make the dance worth your while." He tugs on a piece of my hair that has fallen from hair ponytail affectionately.

"I bet you can." I reply, shooing his fingers away from my damp hair.

"Well, you better not be late for your curfew. Lets get to your van."

"Yeah, I had better." I say. I am exhausted from the game anyways, so going home early will not be a problem. Besides, I have a lot to prepare for still by the dance. I smile to myself as we approach my vehicle. My first dance with a boyfriend, life really is magical.

The next night arrives, and the winter formal is almost upon me. But, I cannot find my purse that matches the dress I bought months in advance for this.

"MOM! Where is my fancy purse?" I am almost ready. Zac is almost here. But, I cannot for the life of me find my purse. "MOM!!!" I am growing frantic, I need to find it. My mother screams up the stairs.

"It is hanging in the closet down here, don't worry!"

Disaster averted. I hear the front door downstairs squeak open, then multiple, loud footsteps heading up the stairs. My friends must have arrived

"Are you ready Ellie?!" Emily, Tara, and Samantha burst into my room. They look gorgeous.

Emily is wearing a short cocktail dress, a deep purple with gemstones covering the torso of the dress. Her dirty blonde hair is pinned back, showing her slender neck.

Tara is wearing a dark green silky dress, the hem falling just short enough to see her black heels. Her hair is falling loosely in curls that must have taken her forever to style.

Samantha is stunning in a hot red dress that looks more fit for a ballroom than a winter dance. Her hair is put up with some waves falling majestically on the side of her face. She is sure to get some attention in that, we all are. I look down at my own dress and hope that I look as pretty as my friends.

"Yep, I am ready. Are our dates meeting us here?" I ask them, unsure of what they have planned.

"They sure are, I believe they will be here any moment." Samantha is stoked for the upcoming night. It is written all over her face. Just as she speaks, the doorbell rings, "They are here!" Tara cries. Time for the night to begin.

We walk down the stairs, my eyes find Colin, Nate, Ryan, and finally they rest on my Zac. They all look very well groomed for this event.

"Well, don't you guys just clean up well?" Samantha teases them, "Especially you." She winks at Colin, and wraps her arm around his, his face blushing.

"You ladies clean up alright yourselves too!" Nate laughs at us.

"Okay enough talking, lets go!" I say, making eye contact with Zac. He smiles at me, I wonder how I look to him.

"WAIT! We need pictures first." My mom runs towards us, and begins lining us up. "Okay, smile." The flash goes off before we are ready, and the continues to go off. Zac's arm is around me, and we are all smiling at the camera. Finally, she is appeased.

"Okay, be safe, don't be home too late." My father warns us. We happily agree, and off we are.

"Okay, pile in! Emily and Ryan you go with Tara and Nate. Zac, El, you are with us!" Samantha leads us to her car, always the one to drive.

"See yah there!" I wave to Emily and Tara as we get into our vehicles, time to go.

Zac clambers into the back seat beside me, and our eyes lock, "You know you look absolutely stunning, Ella."

I hear Samantha giggle in the front, oblivious to us, her concentration on driving and the boy sitting beside her. My cheek brighten, did I mention what I am wearing? My dress is a short golden dress, the sparkles reflecting in the car lights. My short brown hair, slowly growing out from my blonde short hair phase the previous year is in a ponytail, my hair pulled away from my face.

His finger caresses my cheek, and it makes me heart flutter.

"Thanks, you look pretty sexy yourself. Even not matching."

I smile at him, he looks adorable in his khakis and blue shirt that do not match my dress at all, but works for us nonetheless.

"Yeah, sorry about that." He reaches back to scratch his head anxiously.

"Don't worry, it works." I grab his hand down, and hold it in mine. And it does work. Everything is working for me tonight. I feel ready to let go of my worries, no need to let future events bring me down.

We arrive at the dance, and the night begins. My friends laughing beside me, we all enter the school where just last night we had played our last basketball game. The gym is packed, but for the dance this time. I look around, the dance is underway, we all make our ways to a table that has not yet been taken.

"Wow, they did this gym up pretty well for this dance." Emily gushes.

"They sure did." My eyes looking around at all the familiar faces, somehow different when done up for this event. The girls all dolled up, and the boys dressed up at their sides. It is beautiful in its own way, how everyone goes all out for something as simple as a dance.

The gym itself is hung with decorations, snowflakes and tinsel lining the beams above us. The lights are darkened, and they even hung up a disco ball to reflect the soft glowing lights. It is beautiful.

"Oh my gosh, they have food!" Nate bellows, and we lose the boys all at once. I regain myself from my own thoughts, I almost follow them to the food and punch table, but Samantha grabs my arm.

"Whoa now, hey boys grab us some punch!" She yells at them, and then turns back to us, "Look at what I have got." She opens her purse to reveal (I am assuming) vodka in a water bottle, I am betting this dance is about to get a whole lot better.

"Sammie, you did not!" Emily shakes her head at her friend, always the good one.

"Oh, shush up, you think that Colin doesn't have a fifth for the boys? A little spiked punch never hurt anyone!"

"She is right, who is really going to catch us? The good kids?" Tara says matter of factly.

"I agree, lets do it! Might as well live it up while we are all together." I agree with them, why not have a little bit of fun? I am going to be valedictorian, who would suspect us of drinking? And, besides, who would really care? I need to let loose.

"But…" Emily tries to be the adult, but is interrupted.

"Some punch for our ladies!" Nate mock bows to Tara, and hands her the glass of punch. Zac chuckles, and sits my glass on the table.

"Okay, now for the better part of the punch." Sam removes the vodka from her purse, and pours it into our glasses, more vodka than punch.

"Oh my gosh, lets just get hammered as soon we walk in." Emily laughs, "You guys are lucky I am doing this with you just so that we all go down together."

"And to look cool in front of me, right?" Ryan jokes with her, putting his arm around her shoulders. Her face reddens, she is lucky that we are too good of friends to publicly mock her in front of her date.

At that moment, Zac grabs my hand in his under the table and squeezes. I turn to face him, his eyes already on mine.

"I think I hear our song, would you like to go dance?" He asks me, unknowing about my dance moves, or lack thereof. But, what am I supposed to do, turn down this handsome boy? Or hope that he does not know how to dance either? Cross my fingers for the latter.

"Why, I would love to." I almost giggle at the end, but restrain myself. How dare I let this kid turn me into another ditzy female who cannot control her outbursts when around him. My friends can all see through me though, I am taken by Zac, even when my thoughts stray to Byron. Which, by the way, I wonder where he is? No, no. Dance time.

Zac escorts me to the dance floor (gym floor, obviously), it is a slow song. The kind where everyone leaves the floor, and then slowly drifts back as couples holding each other's hands. Me, being one of them for once.

Nate and Tara, Ryan and Emily, Samantha and Colin, all follow suit behind us. Zac places his hands on the side of my hips, as mine loop around his shoulders. We slowly begin moving, shuffling to the music. He is not a bad dancer at all, but how would I know? Well, he isn't stomping on my feet anyways.

"How are you liking the dance so far?" I ask him, lifting my head to meet his eyes. His eyes are so blue, as deep and calm as the ocean. I feel like I could look in his eyes forever. It is almost like I can feel my heart thudding within my chest, is this what young love feels like? Have I been over complicating my feelings this entire time? It could be, I would like for it to be that way. My reeling of thoughts does ruin things more often than not, like right now.

"I think that I like it a bit more than usual, because I am with you. You look so beautiful, Ella. I want you to know that, you are gorgeous and I love you." He loves me.

"I love you too Zac, you are perfect." And, I mean that. I really do. He is the boy of my dreams, the one that I would think about as a little girl. A gentleman, my gentleman.

I wonder what we are going to do after we graduate. We haven't even talked about the future, I barely even like thinking about it. I need to get rid of these nagging thoughts, live in the moment for once.

"Haha, I am glad you think that." He chuckles at me, "And, I love how you blush whenever you tell me your feelings." He leans down and kisses my nose lightly. I can't help but agree with him, I have never been good with my feelings. I suppose over thinking goes hand in hand with having troubles bearing your feelings.

"Yeah, never been one to bear my feels, yah know? Not very good at it." I can't believe I just admitted that, told him about my feelings. I suppose that is what significant others do, tell each other things. I think I just called them the feels though, using my own slang, way to go Ella.

"You think I haven't realized that? Haha." I chuckle with him, brushing my hair back from falling in my face. I lean my head on his shoulder to enjoy the remainder of this song.

Then, I spot Byron across the room, just entering the dance, an hour late. But, a girl is with him. Who is she? She faces my direction, and I see it is that mousy girl, Rebecca from Colin's party a while back. Well, at least he didn't take that annoying sophomore I told him to. Although, I cannot help but feel a twinge of jealousy.

I have a boyfriend, one I love. Why does it matter whom my best friend brings to the dance? Perhaps, he did it out of kindness. It doesn't matter anyways.

He looks good, he got a haircut and is wearing all black. He looks like he could be the king of darkness, his jet black hair matching his clothes, even his tie is black. His pale skin almost illuminated by the darkness of his shirt, his eyes reflecting every light in the dance. His date beside him matched in all black as well, I almost can not help but admit that they look quite the couple. Leave it to him to know how to make an entrance without even trying.

He sees me looking, and waves at me. The song is almost over, Zac and I break apart. Instead of going to greet him as he expects, I go back to the table to my friends already sitting, drinking their spiked drinks.

"Who wants to go grab everyone cookies from the food table?" Samantha asks, loud as usual. I see her punch glass is already gone, she must have chugged it, mine still sits untouched. I go for it, and slam it. The warm vodka and punch make me choke, my throat tightening in gag reflex, but I choke it down without more than a grimace.

"Woah! Ella is in the spirit!" Colin downs his cup, and slams it on the table as well. Soon everyone is following suit, we are all cheering each other on.

"Haha, I will go grab us some cookies." I say, and get up to leave the table and my laughing friends.

Zac looks after me, "I can grab us all some punch", he gets up to follow me.

"Looks like someone is planning on a fun night." He jostles my arm.

"Yeah, maybe. Need to celebrate our great year. I mean, it has been a pretty good senior year so far and we will all be graduating in a couple of months, it is crazy. I cannot even wrap my head around my looming adulthood." I throw my arms out in exaggeration to get my point across.

"Is someone already feeling a bit tipsy?"

"Psh, noooo. Get that pitcher and fill it with some punch for our table, punch boy."

"I am punch boy now? Beer bitch, punch boy. Your flirting needs a little work." He winks at me, and puts his hand against my back.

"Hey now, it got you didn't it?" I push him away and put my hands on my hips.

"Haha, yeah I guess it did." He starts filling the cups with punch.

I start filling the plates with the different food that is also available, man, they really went all out. They have cookie, pretzel, and other snack assortments. I don't even know where to start, my stomach growling from not eating all day. Whenever I am nervous, I forget to eat, a poor habit I should probably break.

"Okay, I am going to head back to the table with the punch before they come after me." Zac turns to go, and I nod my head at him still shoving the plate full of pretzels, cookies, and chips. He laughs at my mouth full of an Oreo, and turns to head back to the table.

I go to grab another plate to ladle with food, and Byron appears by my shoulder.

"Hey Ella, hungry?" He laughs at me, and grabs a cookie to eat.

"Ha, yeah, you know me, never full. You look nice, I am glad you came." I nod my head at him, giving him an appreciative look.

"Thanks, and you look really nice too, Ella."

"Aw, thanks for the false flattery, who is your date?" I turn to to shake my head in the direction of his date. Even though, I already know who it is.

"Oh her? You remember Rebecca from that party, right? She asked me, and I didn't see why not since all my other friends were going with a date." He shrugs.

"Cool, cool. Well, Samantha has some vodka over at our table if you are interested in a little more of a party."

"She would, yeah, mind if Rebecca sits with me too?"

I roll my eyes, "Yeaaaah, your little freshman is welcome. Just don't sit her next to Samantha, she may bite." I joke with him, and he returns my look with a deadpan gaze, then laughs so I know he gets that I am kidding.

"Yes, I know. I will be over to your table in a bit." He quickly hugs me, winks at me, and heads back over to his date with her punch.

I grab my plates and heads towards our table. I can't believe that girl got the courage to ask him to the dance, that is ballsy. Kind old Byron would take her, of course. That makes sense. I am glad he it out for the night, and actually smiling. I had started to miss my friend's old dry humor.

"So, don't get all queen of the school on me, but I invited Byron and Rebecca to sit with us a little later." I say, specifically to Samantha.

She gives me a mock shocked face, "Why would I mind?!"

"Oh you know, your whole underclassmen thing." Colin nudges her, then flicks a chip at Ryan. Ryan laughs, and throws one back.

"I know of no such thing!" She accuses us, pouring more vodka into her drink.

"Sure you don't." Emily jeers in her direction.

"Well, I do not mind, sheesh." Samantha crosses her arm and pouts, conversation over. I reach over and grab the water bottle from her, pouring more into my punch.

"Dang El, you should probably slow down if you want to remember the dance." Tara scolds me. I see her mom look forming, and I stick out my tongue at her. Tonight I intend on forgetting every anxious thought that typically consumes me. No future thoughts, no Byron, just the night. I can be a good time too.

"Real mature Ella." Tara sticks her tongue back at me. I continue to pour the vodka into my punch, half and half.

"I just want to have some fun!" I whine, "I mean, you only live once, right?" I start drinking my punch, slower this time, the last drink still lingering in my throat. Tara sighs at me, and lets me continue drinking.

"I love this song, lets go dance!" Tara shouts, grabbing the closest person's arm to drag them to the dance floor. Poor Emily was the nearest, she gives Tara a pleading look. "Nope, you are dancing. Anyone else want to join?" She asks all of us.

"Oh, why not. Lets go for it." Samantha says, and grabs my arm. Looks like I am being forced to dance as well, I may need some more vodka for this. I grab the cup and bring it to the dance floor with me, the boys follow us. Time to start shaking what my mama gave me, Samantha would kill me if I said that out loud, what am I, 50?

The music is pulsating, and I continue drinking, before long I can feel the vodka starting to kick in. Samantha must feel it too because she is drinking straight out of the water bottle now, I snatch it from her and take a chug, then chase it with my already vodka loaded punch.

All I can feel is the moment, the sweat forming at the edge of hairline, I wipe it away. My feet find the beat, we are all dancing together. My vision is swirling, I need to go back to the table. I tap Tara and point to the table, she follows suit, and we all head back to the table excluding Samantha and Colin who are too lost in each other to notice.

"Woo, I was getting a little dizzy, I do not know how Sam does it…" I plop into my chair, Emily replies, "Me either, she is crazy!"

Tara giggles, "I think I am tipsy." She leans on Ryan, and they begin canoodling. I turn my attention to Zac, "Having fun?!" I say a little too loudly, I think I echoed a bit.

"I am having a great time! You?" He flashes his pearly whites at me, they are so white. How is he so pretty? Oh my gosh, my head is already spinning. I may not make it to the after party celebrating the start of winter break.

"Great!" I smile at him, so he believes that I am not feeling sick, even though I am. "I am actually going to head to the bathroom real quick, I will be right back!"

I stumble to the bathroom, past the chaperones who eye me warily, not wanting to do more work than they have to. I am almost there.

"Ella, you okay?" I hear a voice to the right of me.

Who is asking me that? I see Byron standing with his hand on the girl's shoulder who is talking, Rebecca. His date. Duh.

"Oh, I am fine, don't you worry about me, just need to use the ladies room." I slide past them before Byron can give me his all knowing look. I rush into the stall, and puke. I knew I should not have drank that much so quickly, I am a light weight. I hear a knock on my stall.

"Ella, you okay?" Byron calls from the other side. I can hear the girls giggling in the restroom, quickly exiting due to this male intruder. The embarrassment!

"I am fine, go away!" He cannot hear me puking.

"Okay, I will wait outside." He is determined.

I hear him leave the restroom, I flush the toilet and sit on the floor. He is such a good friend it is almost obnoxious, magically appearing when I am in need. He makes me so angry.

I think I feel better now, nothing a little puke up can't fix. I head to the mirror to fix my make up, thank gosh I found my purse or I would not be able to fix this puke stained face.

"You feeling better?" Byron is leaning against the wall outside the bathroom when I exit, his date nowhere in sight.

"Yeah, I am. Where is your date?"

"She went to dance with her friends. You think I would let her hang out here to witness you puking?" He pats my arm, "Little too much alcohol?" He knows, he always knows, I must be so predictable. I hug my arms to my chest, "Maybe..."

"I figured. Ready to head back into the dance?" He knows that I will not want to discuss it any further, our silent understanding lingers in the air.

"Fine, lets go." He follows me back into the gym, where everyone is still sitting at the table, drinking. Just because I puked, does not mean that I am down for the count. I pick up a cup and begin nursing myself back to drunken health.

"Woah there Ella, slow down a bit or you will be too drunk for the after party!" Samantha warns me. I really must not drink a lot for even Samantha to be watching my alcohol intake. This good girl persona I have seriously needs to end. I take another chug and look at the table.

"Oooh, I will be fine." And, I will be. Puking really leaves room for more. Byron is shaking his head at me from across the table, his date beside him, swooning all over him.

"Nice, where is the after party?" Rebecca chimes in, and Byron responds before Samantha can get to her. "It is at Colin's place, like usual."

"Great, can I come?" She asks Colin.

"Sure, everyone is invited." He replies nonchalant, Colin never has cared about who comes to his parties, as long as they do not cause trouble.

"Awesome! I will go let my friends know!" She jumps from the table, off to tell her friends of her invite to the Senior party. Of course.

Tara rolls her eyes at us, "You guys ready to get out of here?"

"Sure am." Samantha says, "I am almost out of vodka!"

"Same, let's go. Everyone got extra clothes?" We all nod our heads, no sense in ruining our dresses out in the boonies.

"Are you going to come Byron?" I turn to him.

"Yes, I don't see why not. I am sure my friends will be coming."

"Cool, see you there!" We all head out for the night.

This is where the real magic begins. The party is already underway by the time we get there, Colin having gone straight there with Samantha to set things up while the rest of us took our time changing and grabbing more food at the store to take there. The amount of people that have showed up is almost ridiculous, I am so glad that the party is inside his heated barn this time. The weather has been dropping now that December has hit.

The barn is almost like a large garage, with windows and even a mini kitchen. Leave it to him to have the setup, there is even a beer stand set up in the corner of the room with multiple kegs and other choice drinks. I grab Zac, and head over to the beer stand to get started, although my steps are already a bit wobbly.

"Hang on there Tiger, let's take a break for a moment." He says to me. Take a break? I do not think so. My thoughts are too blurred to process anything except the conflicts surfacing in my head, the result of my overthinking. Why did Byron bring another girl to the dance, what was wrong with me? Why was I thinking about him anyway? What am I going to do when I graduate, it is only a couple of months away. My head is spinning, just one more drink.

"Come on, don't be such a party pooper." I whine at him.

"You are lucky you are so pretty." He replies, and laughs at me. "I will go grab us both a beer, how is that?"

"Sounds good to me, I will plop down right here." I motion to the chair beside me, emphasizing my plopping motion.

"Okay, good, I will be right back." I stick out my tongue at him to make him laugh as he walks away.

"Someone a little tipsy?" Emily slides up next to me with Ryan.

"Me? Never." I laugh at my own joke.

"Yeah, that slur of yours means nothing." Ryan says, as Emily smacks him.

"Shhh, no slur here." I giggle just as Zac returns with my beer.

I thank him, and continue my drinking. The remainder of my friends soon join, getting up to mingle and some staying to talk as parties usually go. Zac eventually gets up to go talk with his friends, leaving me alone at the table, the rest of my friends have disappeared somewhere in this mass of an event. Alone at the table, alone with my thoughts. I need some fresh air.

The air is chilly, it has started off as a mild winter, so it is not quite as brisk as it tends to get towards the end of December. It is perfect, my sweater keeps me warm. I choose this moment to relax and breath in the night air. I am not ready to grow up, it scares me. None of my friends seem to notice that their lives are about to change, am I the only one able to acknowledge it? No, Byron has. I can see it in the way that he has been acting out; stealing, smoking weed, freezing me out with the smallest of arguments.

He is afraid, and this is how he protects himself. I can see it. He tries to hide it, but I know my best friend. He is unsure of his future, as I am unsure of my own. Graduating high school is a big deal, it is the moment where you enter the world on your own. What am I doing to do? I do not even know which college I want to attend, let alone what I want to do for the rest of my life. This is so complicated, I just want to enjoy the last moments of being kid. Drinking and dancing with not a worry in the world.

"Little cold out, isn't it?" Byron sneaks up on me.

"Did you just get here?" I ask.

"Yeah, I was about to head in to the party when I saw you out here. What are you thinking about?"

I debate on if I should tell him or not. That I was thinking about him, about my future, and the scary world that resides outside this town. Maybe ask him why he is acting so strange, to strengthen my assumptions on my own thoughts.

Drunk me speaks before I can even complete more of my thoughts, oh the joys of alcohol. "My future, life. I think I know why you have been acting out these past few months. It is scary to grow up, don't you think?"

I can almost feel his sigh next to me, "Yes, growing up can be scary Ella, you got me." His tone tells me otherwise, I push farther, something I have never done.

"I am not sure if I am ready. Don't tell me that you are fine and that I got you, what is wrong?" I ask him.

"Well, it is coming soon, whether you are ready for it or not. Unless you can find a way to escape it. Sometimes, I want to escape it." The sadness in this statement is audible. My best friend is depressed, how have I not seen it this whole time?

"Maybe we can find a time machine and travel back in time together." I nudge him, "We can invent something great, then be rich and famous by the time we arrive at this exact time again. Perhaps find the Fountain of Youth while we are at it!" I try to cheer him up.

He chuckles at me, a laugh, always a good sign. "Oh, Ella. You always know how to lighten my mood, I love you for that."

"And, I love you for always being a grumpy gills." I chide at him. "And, for being my rock. You are always there for me, thank you." My sentimental drunk side comes out a bit.

I can see his teeth shining in the darkness as he laughs at me. "Oh Elly Belly, you are the best friend I could have asked for." There it is again, best friend zoned. Before my drunken self can comprehend what I am about to do, I lean up to kiss him. On. The. Lips.

I can feel him recoil, but slowly he relaxes and kisses me back for only a moment. A moment was all I ever needed, a moment to hold on to.

"Ella…" I know what he is about to say, that I am his friend and that I have Zac. Zac. Whose feelings I did not consider, but I will not back down before I have my say.

"Someday, I will make you love me in the way that I love you."

"Ella, you will understand me eventually."

"I know I will. Byron, will you promise me one thing?" I look up at him, holding him to his spot.

I can feel his breath on my cheek, "yes, anything Ella."

"Promise me you will never hurt yourself, that you will get over this… If not for yourself, but for the people that love you, like me. I just love you so much and I could never imagine a world without you. Do you love me too? I know you do, you have to feel it too."

For what seems like an eternity, Byron says nothing. Then, he looks down at me, and a tear slides down his cheek. Before I realize what is happening, he grabs my face and kisses me. He kisses me with the past seven years of love and friendship, the confusion and the pain. I kiss him back, the fire between us threatening to burn us alive.

But then, he releases me. "I do love you, but I can never be what you need." With that, he walks away. I don't even breathe, not wanting to comprehend my own feelings.

Why must he always respond with such cryptic answers?

Also, what have I done? I cheated on my first boyfriend. No, I did not. I will not count this against myself, no one will know. Byron will not say anything, he is too embarrassed by what we have done. Time to face myself for the rest of this party, and my guilty conscience. I hope Byron is okay.

"Ella! Where have you been?" Zac greets me as I re-enter the barn. I smile at him before responding in my drunken stupor. I grab my cup and continue drinking.

If only I could love him in the way that he loves me. But, I cannot help whom I love. The only future I can see is one with my Byron, I know he will love me someday. He just needs time to sort through his own feelings.

And, no these are not the thoughts of a stalker. Byron does love me, he is just too into his teenage angst to recognize what kind of love it is yet. I have known him since we were kids, he can't see me as anything else yet. Someday...

Chapter 7

$\mathcal{I}$t has been a week since I last saw Byron, I keep calling him but I have the feeling that he is ignoring me, but I don't understand why. He said he loved me, I love him too. We can work this out. I can't help but continuously play it over in my head though, he seemed so sad. In my drunken state, I had not realized how sad my friend seemed, so far away from reality. I want to help him.

It has been bothering me ever since, his sadness. How had I not seen it before? Byron was depressed, I knew it now, and I need to talk to him about it. If only he would answer my phone calls, I pick up the phone and try one more time.

"Hello?"

To my relief, it is Byron. "Hey! Merry Christmas Eve, or however that goes."

"Oh, hey Ella. Sorry about ditching you this break, I have just been really busy."

I know he is lying, but I want to talk to him in person, so I bite my tongue. "That's okay, what are you doing today? Want to exchange gifts?" I know this will get him, because tomorrow is Christmas.

"Yeah, I can do that. I will be home all day, so just swing on by."

"Okay, sounds good. I will see you soon…" I want to say more, but the dial tone clicks before I can. Sometimes, he can be such an asshole without meaning to. Well, better start getting around if I want to bombard Byron with my gift and lecture. I want to tell him so many things, but helping him comes first.

"Do you like it?" I almost can't hold it in as Byron opens his present, a dark blue t-shirt sporting the band he had me listen to, Owl City.

He laughs at me, "I love it, Ella. Here is yours." He passes me over a small little box, I tear it open without remorse. A small pair of purple, beaded earrings are inside.

"Oh, I love them, Byron, thank you!" I swoop in to hug him before he can change his mind on my incoming display of affection. He wraps his arms tightly around me as I hoped he would, and we pull back too soon. His eyes are glistening with that sadness I finally see clearly now, now that I am over my selfious nature.

I put my hand on his, "Byron, are you okay? Like, REALLY, okay? I can see how sad you are, I hope you are okay…"

He looks at me, but doesn't see me, not in the way that I know him. "I am fine, Ella. Don't you worry, okay?"

I sigh at him, "Byron, I know you. And, something is wrong."

"Nothing that is fixable."

"What does that even mean?" I can't help but start to get angry with him and his cryptic sayings.

"It means what I just said. There is nothing that you can fix about this, you can't help me"

I want to break down and cry, my best friend is changing so much, and I don't know what to do. "Byron, please let me in…" I whimper at him, trying to hold back my whine.

"There is nothing to let in! I am sad, I am confused, but I will get over it okay?"

He says what he knows that I want to hear. "Are you sure? You would never do anything stupid would you?" A tear escapes and slides down my face, and Byron's gaze softens.

He leans in and hugs me further, "No, Ella. I promise I would never do anything stupid."

I hug him tighter, "Okay, I don't know what I would do without you. I love you."

He whispers in my hair, "I know, Ella, I know." We stay like that for I don't know how long, until it is time for me to leave. To go home, and spend the rest of Christmas Eve with my family. I leave happy, full of love for my best friend, and the paths that we both must choose someday.

It is December 27th, 2009. Christmas has passed, break is halfway over. Practice starts up again next week, though I do not really want to go. I mean, what are the chances that we make the championships?

For Christmas, I got everything that I asked for- a new laptop and a new pair of winter boots. Zac got me a pretty heart shaped necklace, and I got him a movie. I have not yet spoken to him about my kiss with Byron, but I am waiting until the moment is right, whenever that will be. I want to talk with Byron about it first also, clear out the air.

I got Samantha, Emily, and Tara all best friend picture frames with photos of us inside. I haven't spoken to Byron since our gift exchange, but I plan on calling him today, to see how his Christmas was and everything. I am not really sure why I am awake right now, I woke up early for some reason, out my of dead sleep. Perhaps it is just my nerves on the nearing of break's end which means telling Zac, and being one step closer to graduation.

Ring Ring Ring My phone goes off, surprising my morning thoughts.

Geez, who is calling me this early? 6am? Isn't this supposed to my winter break? My first weekend in.

Emily. Figures.

I almost throw my phone back down, but something stops me.

"Whyyyyy are you calling me so early?" I moan.

"Ella, something has happened…" Her despair is evident through the phone. She begins to sob. I begin to panic.

"What is it Emily? Are you okay? What is going on?" I am wide awake now, holding my breath. I have a strong feeling in my chest, constricting.

Her sobs begin to subside, choking on her own spit she begins, "You know how Ryan's dad works for the fire station? There has been an accident. I needed to tell you before the news spreads."

"WHAT IS IT, EMILY?"

"Byron was hit by a train." What? Who? It sinks in. Byron. Hit. Train. I cannot process this.

"Well, is he okay? What happened Em? Is he okay? Was he in his car?" He has to be okay. I just saw him a couple of days ago. He was fine. Perfect. We exchanged gifts.

No. I can't even think properly.

"I don't know El... That is all he would tell me. Ella?"

The phone has slid out of my hands. I can only hear her echo on the ground. Who will know more? I need to know more.

John. My brother. He will know. Byron's older brother is his best friend. Good thing winter break is here, so he is home.

I run to his room. "JOHN! JOHN! WAKE UP! CALL BYRON'S BROTHER NOW. NOW! JOHN!" I begin sobbing before my words are all out.

"Ella? What? What is wrong? Ella?" John fumbles frantically out of bed, and grabs his cell phone. "I have 10 missed calls from Brad..." Byron's brother. My heart sinks.

"CALL HIM BACK!" I scream at him. John has no time to respond, he puts the phone to his ear.

"John, what is....?" Moments pass as the other line speaks. My brother's face drains, as he stares at me. Something is terribly wrong. He must be hurt badly... I should go to see him. My brain will not let me register the alternative. NO.

The conversation is over, my brother can't look at me.

"John? Tell me." I am panicking, I cannot feel anything.

His eyes tell me before he does, "Ella, Byron didn't make it." No. No. NO. Am I screaming out loud, or has my mind fused with my mouth. I am wailing. Like a wounded animal. I lunge for my brother, punching him. Slapping. This can't be true.

"YOU LIAR! LIAR! NO!" Brad and John are playing a cruel joke on me, Emily knows too. NO. Arms encircle me, wrapping me tight. John is whispering into my hair, I am fading. My parents must be up by now. Reese is staring at me. I must look a rabid animal. He is scared. I am scared too.

"Ella? His family needs us, they want to see us. Will you come?" John is smoothing my hair. I have fallen into his arms. A doll. Lifeless. My parents and brother surround me, cocooning me in. Letting me cry into the morning light. John fills them in as I cry into his arms.

"You don't have to go if you don't want to Princess." My father caresses my arm.

Do I want to go? Yes. I need to know for sure. I need to see for myself. I need to.

"No. I am going." I say. They say nothing. John takes charge and order me to put on some clothes. I numbly retrieve my jeans and put my hair up, grabbing my glasses with no time to put in my contacts.

We leave.

"Ella, you need to pull yourself together for his family. They need us to be the strong ones right now." John states it. He is not telling me stop mourning; he is not scolding me. Simply stating a fact. I nod. I know this. It is his family. They lost their son; their brother. My best friend is gone, but I need to do this.

I wipe the snot from my nose, there is no fixing my face. It is red and blotchy, swollen from tears and my lips chapped from screaming. I do not want to speak ever again. Or think. I cannot bring myself to think either. This blur of events makes no sense to me. I am thankful for my glasses, they at least help to hide my bloodshot eyes. I keep my mind blank, like a chalkboard that has been erased.

We arrive. Too soon. I need to move. But moving requires work, and I am like a doll. I can do this, John helps me from the car and we walk towards Byron's house. The home that I grew up in, with the comfort of my best friend. I stop thinking once more, I need to hold it together.

We enter the war zone. Brad sees John. John moves towards him, and wraps his arm around his sobbing friend. Brad lost his brother today. I am frozen. Mrs. Rood sees me. Her eyes hold no malice today, her eyes hold a broken mother. I try not to cry once more, but a mother always knows.

Mrs. Rood engulfs me in her arms, "Oh Ella... Our Byron." She weeps to me, I hold her tight. Our feuding gone, forever, in one moment of time. Pain forever bringing us together. Loss of love.

"Do you know what happened?" Mrs. Rood retracts herself from me.

"No..." I whimper. He promised he wouldn't... I feel like a black hole is engulfing me.

"Ella, Byron left a note." A note? How could he leave a note? My worst fear is true. His promise was nothing.

"A note?" It finally registers with me, that this was no accident.

"Yes, would you like to read it?" She is letting me into her moment. She motions me to the table. A legal pad is sitting there. I have always hated legal pads. I hate them even more right now.

His note.

To everyone,

    I don't know what to tell you. I am sorry. No. That is a lie. I am not sorry. I feel pain wherever I am. I am tired of being alive. I want to die. Life is hard, and it is time for me. I know this may come as a shock to you, but I chose this.

    Mom and Dad, I love you. Don't think that I didn't. This isn't your fault. Never think that. Brad, live enough for both of us bro.

    Jerry and Rick, hey guys. Don't hate yourself for this. You made my time here worthwhile.

    Ella, love someone who will love you like I never could...

Byron.

That is it? THAT IS IT? ONE LINE? FOR ALL OF US? How could he do this... NO NO NO. My sadness is overwhelmed with the anger I now feel. HE LEFT ME. HOW COULD HE LEAVE ME? LEAVE HIS FAMILY?

"Ella, he did love you." Mrs. Rood comforts me, even when the hole in her heart is far greater than mine ever could be. My eyes try to find comfort in hers, I cannot. It is not there. I turn and run, run down the stairs to his room. He will be there.

I jerk open the door. Empty. His clothes all over the floor, his chair pulled out. So organized, yet so messy at the same time. He is gone.

My knees give out from under me, I fall to his floor. Weeping. My hands fall on his sweater, his cross country sweater. I giggle, the irony. He hated cross country, he joined it for me… I bring his sweater to my nose and inhale. It is dirty. It smells like him. I clench it to my chest and inhale, again and again.

I hear footsteps behind me, a hand on my shoulder. I grasp it.

"Hey Ella." I don't even need to turn.

"Hey Brad." He falls next to me. He turns and sees the sweater I hold close to me. He grabs a shirt off the ground as well. He inhales, and tears escape, sliding down his face.

"For such a neat freak, his room was always dirty." Was. Brad uses past tense.

"Yes, it was. I am sorry, Brad." My mouth searches for the right words, but none form, they sound wrong. He understands.

"John and I used to joke that you and Byron were meant to be. We made a bet on when he would see it." He chokes on his own laugh, "I guess we will never know now…"

The silence fills the room, I lean my head on his shoulder. We find comfort in each other.

The day is endless. But, it passes through my haze. We go to the funeral home to identify the body. His parents go in. They come out. They do not recommend anyone else see the mess of his body. My Byron. Just a body now. His soul gone from this life.

He laid in front of the train. They tell us. The initial collision did not kill him, the end of the train hitting his head did it. He suffered. The train crushed his leg before he died. He felt the pain. He shit himself. Death is not the romantic ordeal we all imagine.

Death is horrible. It is pain. It is darkness. He had his headphones in, he was listening to his ipod. The train came at 2 am. What was he doing? He said that he would be okay. HE PROMISED ME. I don't understand. Why was he at the tracks at 2am? Why? My heart is breaking as I remember our kiss, our conversation. It is too much, this can't be real.

I try to relive our last day together, but I am too exhausted to even think.

My brain can only register clips. Certain words. Why? No. It clicks on. Click.

Click.

Click.

I wish I could shut it off.

Shut it all off.

I am home again. My friends are here. Friends that I didn't know I had.

Why are they all here? I hear their conversations, but I am not a part of them. Rick and Jerry are here too. They act as I do. I am glad they are here. They understand my pain.

My house seems to be the rendezvous for the grieving. I bet Emily, Samantha, and Tara took over. My parents lets them do what they want. There are no rules today. Kids from my class are here. There is food. I hear them talking. Talking to each other, talking to me. Crying. I hear distant cries. I sit in my room as the people come in and try to talk to me. I say nothing. There is nothing to say.

Byron's date from the dance is here too. How did she know where I live? It doesn't matter.

Zac is here. He attempts to console me. I shut him down. Shut him out. I do not want him here. I do not want anyone here. I want to be alone.

Click.

Click.

I am in my room. It is still day. I thought it would be over by now. But life continues. I hear people downstairs. I locked my door. They know. I need to be alone.

I have his sweater. Brad let me take it. I hold it. Not wear it. I want the smell to linger. The smell of him.

I can't register this. It hurts. It hurts so much. I can't hold it in, my body shakes. It shakes.

"Byron..." His name sounds familiar on my lips, I need him here.

Only my best friend can help me. But. He can't be here. He left me. He lied to me. There is nothing that can help me. Nothing. No one. I am Hell alive, it consumes me.

I cannot sleep. I cannot eat. I simply drift.

Knocking brings me to. I was not sleeping. Simply being. Taking up empty space.

I open the door. My mom wants to come in. I shake my head, no. I do not want anyone. Can she bring me anything? Food? Drink? Comfort?

No. I want nothing. She is at a loss. My mother does not know how to comfort this pain for me. She knows this. She leaves me be.

Byron. Why would you leave me?

Why?

Click.

Night relieves me, the darkness soothes me in its terror. I wonder if he can hear me.

"Byron... Why would you leave me? You promised you would never leave me. Why did you? How could you do this? I am so torn between my love for you and my hate for you. I hate you. Hating you is easier than admitting a piece of my heart is gone. I do not know what to do... WHY?"

I don't know what else to say. Thinking only hurts me. He isn't here. He is dead. Gone. Forever. I solidify it in my mind.

Dead. It is logical. A being simply stops. Death. That is what it is. It happens to everyone at some point. Logic. I can hold onto the logic of it. It helps my pain. I begin doing math in my tired mind, simple then moving to complex. Logic.

Eventually, without knowing, I drift into a fitful sleep.

"Ella.... Help me!" He screams, falling. Byron. He is reaching for me, he is still here. I can save him. I need to only reach him. I cannot extend my hand far enough, he is falling. "Ellaaa..... His voice echoes away. NOO!!! NOO!!!!

I wake to my father holding me tight. I am still screaming. My cries breaking the night.

"Oh Ellie, it is just a nightmare...." My father rocks me, holding me like when I was just a baby.

I am a baby again. Curled into his arms, he can protect me, but not from this. His face is torn from the pain he sees. "Princess, I am so sorry. I am so sorry..."

I cannot stop sobbing. I curl further into my rock, this pain is unbearable. "Dad, it hurts. It hurts so much…" I cry into his shirt, my snot leaving residue behind.

"I know sweetheart, I know." Time doesn't move.

I can hear them downstairs through my vent. I have not moved in days. They are worried for me. They do not know what to do.

I pity them. I pity their confusion. But, I do not want to move. Time does not exist where I am. Zac has called. Emily. Tara. Samantha. So many times. They keep calling. I keep ignoring. They tried to show up. I had my parents send them away. They are worried too. I am not handling this well.

I am not as strong as they thought I was. I am weak. And, I have given up. My door opens.

"Hey Ella." Reese stands there. Reese has not bothered me yet. He has left me alone. I wonder what he wants. I look at him, but I make no attempt to speak. He takes this as his opening. "I wanted to make sure you are okay. You look terrible." He is sincere. I nod at him, withdrawn. I imagine I look terrible.

"Everyone is worried about you. I know you are hurt Ella. But, just know that you have people who love you and are here for you. Always." He stands there, awkwardly. I say nothing. He turns to leave.

Then turns once more. "I love you Ella, and I am sorry. I am here for you." Then he is gone.

Click.

Time passes.

"Ella, get your ass out of bed, we are going to lunch!" Emily slams open my door. My parents looking guilty behind her, they must have invited her here.

I stare back at her. I don't want to talk. She stares back, hard. I lower my eyes. She sighs, and begins digging through my drawers.

She tosses a pair of pants to me, and a sweater.

"If you do not put those on right now, so help me, I will dress you myself." Her gaze is fiery.

"Fine." I say. Slowly, I begin pulling my pants on. I throw on the sweater. She throws my sneakers to me. I insert my feet into them. They feel odd. Everything feels odd.

"And, put your hair up, it looks disgusting." She is not dealing with pleasantries.

I love Emily. I do not need kindness right now, I need someone to tell me what to do; how to continue. Take away my thought process. I tie my hair up, when was the last time I brushed it?

"Okay, let's go to lunch. I am driving. I will follow you out."

"I don't want to." I state.

"I do not give a fuck what you want. You are done moping. Now get up. NOW." I obey. Not because I am afraid of her, but because I do not care enough to argue.

"Great!" She claps her hands. We are off.

"Ella? You aren't eating. Come on…. At least try, you look terrible." Her tone has softened. She wants me to feel better, but I can't.

"I am sorry, I am just not hungry." I mumble. I am sorry.

"You are skin and bones, and you look like you haven't eaten in days. So, eat. You have to move on eventually, Ella. Maybe not now, but you need to try. Everyone is worried about you. Zac won't stop calling me about you. News about you…."

"I don't care." I don't. It is that simple. She looks shocked. I am different. I know that I am. My innocence is gone. Driven away. I no longer care about faking the person I am. I hate everyone, let them know it. If there is a God, I hate him too.

"Ella. Please…. Talk to me at least." She is pleading with me.

"I don't know what to talk about… I can't move on, I can't even think, Emily. My best friend just Goddamn killed himself. HE KILLED HIMSELF."

I want to say more. I want to tell her the guilt I feel for not seeing it, the signs I should have seen. That I blame myself more and more everyday. That I cannot live with myself. I want to tell her how much I loved this boy, my beautiful boy. How we kissed, and about our promise. But, I can't. I can't bring myself to reveal my true emotions. They are mine. If she knew, she would see what a horrible person I am for not being able to save him.

"I know, Ella. I know." She has nothing else to say. She begins chatting away about the practices that I have missed, about the end of break coming up in the next few days. She talks to take me away from the only thing that I think about.

Byron.

His smile.

Gone.

Forever.

Times clicks on.

Chapter 8

Byron's viewing is today. We are holding it in the gym, a place that was filled with joy just weeks ago.

His family has asked me to speak. I agreed, but I do not know what to say. I wrote a speech, but it cannot tell them how I really feel. There will be so many people there. Tell them that I will never be able to love Christmas again? That this holiday will only bring me sorrow for the rest of my days?

Everyone is speaking with me. Mulling me with their condolences and care. His father his speaking. So many people have showed up. I can tell that his father is angry with his son. His speech is halting, and filled with anger.

Byron's mother motions me towards the seats designated for the speakers and family. I am not family. I feel uncomfortable here, in my black dress. I bought this dress for the viewing, I will never wear it again. It is itchy, and makes my back sweat. This is why I chose it. Nothing should be comfortable today.

His brother plays the guitar for him, a song. "I Will Follow You Into the Dark" by Death Cab for Cutie. Another song ruined for me. Forever. This day will ruin so many things for me.

Soon, it is my turn. I am so nervous, there must be a 1000 people here, I swear. The entire town has showed up. People do not kill themselves here, nor do the young die. Byron has become the center of this town. I try not to look around me, I avoid the eyes of everyone.

I smooth down my dress, and hold my speech, it crinkles at my touch. All eyes on me. Do they even know me? No. No one does. Here it goes.

I clear my throat, I will get through this.

"Well, there are a lot of stories that I could tell about Byron, but most of them probably wouldn't be as funny to you guys as much as they are to me. Byron was a great guy, I mean I have known him since Brad first came over with his pack of Ramen noodles back in middle school…" I get a couple chuckles, knowing that Brad has always been a picky eater.

I continue,

"At first it started off with me bugging him all the time just to get him to talk to me because I am pretty sure that I scared him a little bit, haha. After that I liked to make him smile or laugh with my dumb jokes, most of the time it just seemed that I annoyed him, but it never really stopped me. Once I got through his shell though, he wasn't really as serious as he seemed to be, I mean, I have even gotten him to sing on video for me."

The chuckles ripple once more, and I force myself to keep going. No thinking.

"It was probably the best thing I have ever seen. Byron was really funny, smart, nice, and a lot of other things. He would always make time to talk to anyone who wanted to talk to him and he helped anyone who needed help. He was even patient with me, when helping with my homework, even when the teachers couldn't deal with me.

Byron was the first person to attend my weekly breakfasts with my grandpa. He only ever missed a couple since we started in the 8th grade, and that was only when we were having our little fights.

He was great, and helped to shape people's lives. He was really smart, I mean he had all A's, trust me I know, because I was always competing with him… Somehow we always knew what each other's grades were."

More laughs from the audience, I wrote this speech to lighten other's moods, but the memories only darken mine.

"Byron and I fought a lot, but that was only because I get a big mouth when I get mad. And he would always forgive me because that is what he did. He always forgave people… Byron was my best friend, maybe not always willingly, but he was always there for me whenever I needed him. When I needed someone to talk to, or just a hug. He was an amazing person, and I am going to miss him a lot. I know everyone else will too…."

I am crying. I can feel it before I notice, I told myself I would not cry. I hear the applause, and I leave the podium. My heart hurts. I sit down. Hands reach out to pat my back, I ignore them. I enter my own world once more, as the viewing goes on. I didn't say what I really wanted to say. That, he was always there for me when I needed him, but I failed him. I was not there for him when he needed me the most.

The viewing ends. There is more food. More people. Why do people always look to food when they feel pain? Does it help them to fill the gaping hole left behind? My stomach rejects food, I am losing weight. Nothing will fill my hole.

My coach approaches me, he hugs me, he holds me. He tells me that this may not be the place, but we have practice next week. That he understands I needed this week off. We need to be prepared. I nod numbly at him, I am in no mood for this reminder that life is still going on. Everyone is invited to stay for food, and discussion. I do not want to be here. I see Zac running towards me, the pain increases.

"Oh Ella, I love you so much." He grabs me, and hold me close.

Then, I remember, it comes flooding back. Kissing Byron. Loving Zac. Being with Zac. It is just too much. NO.

"Zac, I kissed Byron." I say it, knowing it will hurt him. Make him leave me to my isolation. His face contorts, but he does not waiver.

"Ella, I do not care what you did. I love you, and your best friend just died. I am here for you. I will always be here for you." He is defiant.

So I run.

It is all I can think to do. I turn, and I run. I run away from the people. From the food. From the pictures of my best friend staring back at me, his eyes empty. I run.. And, I keep running. Soon, I am at the playground, blocks away. My vision is blurry, and my lungs burn. I realize how cold it is, I did not bring my coat. It feels good.

I find a swing, and collapse upon it. Swinging absently. I hate this life. Why would it take him away from me? It is a darker place that I do not want to be in. I want to die too. I am not strong, I cannot handle this. It is exhausting. Maybe, if I just stay out here, the cold will take me. My lips are beginning to numb, the snow slowly falling. It looks beautiful, the flakes landing on the black of my dress and blending with the white of my skin. My tears freeze before they leave my face.

I hear a crunching, my ears always better than my eyes. A jacket falls on my shoulders, Zac's coat. He silently takes the swing next to mine, and waits for me to speak. Minutes fall between us, I get up to leave. I do not want to speak.

He understands. He leaves me to our silence, and gets up with me.

We make our way back to the school for the remainder of Byron's viewing. "Ella...." He begins before I cut him off.

"Zac, I am in no place for love right now. Our relationship ends here." It is forthright. He was expecting this, I know it. He nods, but remains at my side. Why must he make this so hard? I do not deserve his love, for I am a coward flooded with guilt and pain.

"I understand, Ella. But, I am still here for you." His hand slides into mine.

The comfort feels hollow, but I need it. His warmth fills me with hope. Hope that someday, I will feel okay again. He gently pulls me towards the school, like I am a child. So much has changed in just a week, I cannot function like a normal person anymore. I am now a child that needs their hand held.

Everyone is still talking, eating, laughing at the memories of Byron. Attempting to make this sad occasion one with a little light at the end of the tunnel. I do not join in. Instead, I tell everyone I need the restroom. Zac looks at me unsure, but I make it sound convincing.

Then I leave. I go to my car, and I drive away. I drive to my quiet place. I place that I took Byron to once many years ago, when I was first sharing my soul with his.

It is state land, a wooded area with many paths. The path I take leads to tree, a tree with a small bench underneath it. No one goes there, it is a dead end. A place for people to think. People like me.

It is cold out, I brought my jacket with me this time but my dress is still thin enough to feel the chill, and my legs are exposed to the elements. But, I do not mind. The bench is wet with snow, yet I feel the most comfortable I have in a long time. I let my mind wander to the first time I brought Byron here.

"Ella, where are we going?"

I smile at him, "You will see soon enough!" I pull him along, as he crankily follows.

"Ella, this path is a dead end, come on."

"Okay, we are here." We stop in front of a tree, miles down the path. A lone bench long overgrown in front of it from lack of use. "Nothing is ever a real dead end, my friend. Some just lead to one thing." I plop down on the bench, and pat the seat beside me.

The sun is warm against our skins, summer at its peak, we were about to enter high school. It seemed so scary at the time. I had brought him there to calm his fears. He smiles at me, the sun shining blue against his dark, long hair. It was beginning to cover his eyes, he had to constantly flip it back to be able to see. Puberty had not yet transformed his scrawny body to the dense muscles from his years of sports. But, he was still beautiful to me, he had always been beautiful to me.

What had he said to me, oh yes… He said, "This spot if beautiful, Ella, perhaps people should follow it to the end."

I had been happy, he had been happy. "Well, if more people did, then this would not be my spot, now would it?" I had laughed at him, and we had indulged in only each other's company. Eventually, this spot would become his as well. A shared secret between us.

"Byron, promise me that even as the years go on. We will always have each other, til the end." My feelings for him had not yet blossomed, but they were turning with the seasons. He had laughed at me, and held out his pinky.

"I promise. Always."

My daydream whips away, I am smiling. Then, I remember. It is like a cold shock to the system, remembering that the memory is not only in the past, but the person. I miss him. So much. The tears salt my lips, making them even colder. This place is changed, changed for me.

I finally stop to think. After the clicking of the passing moments, turned off, I relish in this moment. Of peace. Byron's memory washes over me. I should have been there for him, how did I not see the signs? I had let him slide on by as I bathed in my happiness.

I had left him when he needed me the most. And, the worst part? I did not even know that I was needed. That is the part that hurts the most. He had been hiding behind a facade, and I should have known. When he was spiraling, I was oblivious to his darkness.

"You can't fix sadness, Ella." "Everything will make sense eventually, Ella."

He was stealing. He was drinking. He was doing drugs. He was moody and distant. A stage I thought was temporary, became his permanence. This will be something I have to live with for the rest of my life. I had let my best friend down. He no longer had a future. It was gone in a wim.

My parents have decided it is a good idea for me to see a psychiatrist now that a month has passed. They think that I am not coping well, but I think that I am doing just fine. I have done what is required of me, I have been going to practice, I have hung out with my friends a couple of times, I go to school. I do it all. I go through the motions, but I am not there.

At least, I am still here.

How else are you supposed to cope when your best friend chooses to lie down in front of a train? Yep, offs himself. Violent way to picture it, isn't it? It is almost as violent as being told how he died. Death is violent and his choice of death was horrible.

Okay. Maybe it is understandable why they want to me see this doctor, but I only promised one visit to see how I like it.

"One visit, just see how you like it." My mother pleads with me.

"Fine, one." I say it just to make her happy, she doesn't need to be sad with me. Perhaps, I should try harder to put on a fake cheer, it is just so hard.

I can't stop thinking about him.

"Hello, Ella. Would you like to take a seat?" Dr. Whatshisname motions me to a chair, not even a lay down one like in the movies.

What a waste already, I am missing last period for this? One of my favorite classes even, band, where I can lose myself, if only for an hour. Now, that is even being taken away from me.

I sit down.

"My name is Dr. Watts. I am here to talk with you. Would you like to talk about anything, Ella?"

"Not really."

And it is true, I said I would go, not that I would talk about it. I mean, his name is Dr. Watts. How cliche can you get? I almost want him to make a joke about a lightbulb that goes off with his ideas or something, maybe then, I could write him off and just leave.

"Okay, we can start with that. I will start off talking then. Your parents tell me that you have lost someone close with you. Is this accurate information?"

"Yes." Duh.

"How did he pass?

"They didn't tell you?"

"Well, yes, but I would like your point of view on it."

He lies already.

"Okay. He killed himself. He laid in front of a train, and it killed him."

"That is a horrible thing to have to go through, especially at such a young age. It must have really hurt you, him doing that."

"It did. He left me…" I will not cry in front of this man.

Talking about it is too hard, I don't think I can do this without sending waves of sadness throughout me. I need to shut it off, like I do everyday. Logic. I will shut it off with logic, this man will not win over my feelings.

"He left you? Why would you say it like that?"

"Because he did. He left me. He left everyone." A tear escapes from the the corner of my eye. I can feel it sliding down my cheek, I turn away so he cannot see.

"Ella, I know that it hurts. When my grandmother passed, I was in pain too."

Wait. Did he just compare my best friend killing himself at 17 to his frickin grandmother dying? No. Any feelings I might have wanted to discuss are gone.

My logic is back. That was worse than a light bulb joke.

"I am not in pain. He died. It happens to everyone. I am over it."

"Not everything can be so rationalized, Ella. Death is not as simple as a textbook definition."

"Yeah, and neither is comparing your grandmother passing to my 17 year old best friend killing himself. I am sure you feel pain over her loss, but you do not know anything about the way that I feel." With that, I get up and leave. I can say that I tried.

"Ella, your session is not over!" I hear him behind me.

A voice that I no longer have to listen to because I have already given up on this. This man cannot help me. This doctor claiming to know my pain. He doesn't. This was a waste of breath.

I am out of the building, and soon enough I am in my car. Panting from anger. It is only 2:10, I did not even last 10 minutes with the man. I suppose this will not count as one visit with my parents. I have been excused for the rest of the day, and school is still not over. I am not sure what to do with myself.

I choose to just drive. So, I do.

The logical part of my brain still whirring.

I begin to talk, talking to him eases my pain somedays.

"Hey Byron. I know that you may be listening or maybe you are not. I am not so sure what I believe in anymore. I want to say that I forgive you, and that I miss you. But, honestly only one of those is true. I do miss you, but I do not forgive you. I actually think that I hate you quite a bit. And, I am angry with you. REALLY ANGRY.

I think that you are a coward for leaving. I think that you are selfish and I hate you. How could you do this to me? How could you do this to your family, your friends, and everyone who cared about you?

We promised each other that we would always be there for each other. I know that I failed you, but I want you to know that you failed me too. You should have fought harder... You should have. This is too much for me. I am breaking. You have broken me. I need you here, now.

I need you Byron. I loved you so much. You were the light in my life, and now there is a hole in my heart. I would rather hate you, it is so much easier than loving someone who is gone..."

I guess my parents were right, talking does help. Just not the talking that they had in mind. Talking to him, I can almost feel like he is still here with me. Like he is not gone forever.

"I guess talking out loud really does help. It helps me to realize what my feelings are. Sometimes it is easier to talk before thinking, that way I have no way to process it before I hear it. What I am saying is coming straight from my soul. I am so fucking goddamn pissed at you.

Woo, did you hear that? I am cursing at you. And, you know what? You are the bitch, Byron! Not me! I may have pushed your buttons, but I would never have left you! I loved you, you know that. And, all I get it one mother fucking line in your stupid ass suicide note? I deserved better than that, everyone who loved you did!"

My breathing is quickening, I am screaming. I am angry at him, so angry. I need to stop driving. I slow, and park on the side. I am somehow on a dirt road, a couple miles down from my house. I barely remember driving here, I hardly remember which directions I chose.

I scream. Loud. And long. It feels so good to let it out. This is how I need to let my emotions out. I scream again.

And again.

I scream so loud that the cows in the pasture turn to look in my direction. I scream until I can no longer get another word out. My throat is sore, the physical pain blocks my emotions. This trip has helped me.

"Hey Byron, I hope you are happy where you are. Because, I am not." And, I take a deep breath and drive away.

Back home. Where I run into my empty house, and relish in the emptiness of it. The emptiness that I feel matching my surroundings. I make my way up to my room, drudgingly walking up the stairs.

My walls still hold the pink flowered wallpaper that was chosen for me before I had any opinions of my own. My wall holds posters from anime, popular bands, and a painting of an angel that my grandmother bought me before she passed away. My dresser is solid white, with my mattress on the floor. I used to have the tendency of falling off of my bed, so I decided that I did not need one. A mattress was all I ever needed.

Suddenly I hate my room, I hate the brightness of it all. I go to the corner of my wall where the wallpaper has begun to peel from the age of time. I tear on it, a large strips comes off. It is liberating, I begin tearing it all off. The flowers, the pink. I do not want this anymore, I am too old for this.

When my arms ache from the stripping of my walls, I begin tearing my posters down. Green Day, Fall out Boy, Blink-182, Sailor Moon, more cartoons and bands. I do not need these, I reach the painting of my angel. She looks so serene, yet full of sorrow. She will stay...

What now? My emotions blind me to the consequences of any actions from here on, I grab a black marker from my bag. I begin to scribble and draw on my wall. Dark faces, words and poems that I create as I go. My imagination stretches across my walls, the art flows from the marker. It feels so good to draw, drawing my pain away.

Soon, I feel the door open to my room. Reese enters. He stares at me, how I must look to him.

He looks around my newly decorated room, and whistles. "Dang, Ella. Mom and Dad are gonna be pissed at you!"

I can't help it, I laugh. I laugh through my tear stained face, I cannot stop. To think that through all of this, such a normal thing can be said.

"Yes, they will be." Reese's simple words calm me.

We look at one another, and he sees through me. He walks over to me, grabs the marker out of my hand, and writes his name on the wall, then begins to draw around it. "I think you need a little bit of variety on your walls here, my work will help blend yours. Plus, I have always wanted to do this." He chuckles at me, or maybe at himself.

I collapse onto my mattress, and begin to cry. Loud, guffawing cries. Reese stops, and bends down to lift me up. He lifts me like a doll, I have not noticed that he is growing up. He is about a foot taller than me, and he is built large, but strong. He brings my head to his chest, and holds me. I have been coddled by so many people in the last few weeks, but never Reese... Him and I have never had the close relationship that some siblings have. We do not touch each other nor do we show affection, but today, he showed me his love.

He lets me cry, and says nothing. My little brother, he is so strong, I wish that I could be like him.

Soon, I hear a car pull up. My mother must be home. She always arrives before my dad. Reese releases me, and says, "You stay here, I will tell mom. Okay?" My little brother, he feels so much older than me at this moment in time. I nod my head shakily, and wipe my eyes on my sleeve. He smiles at me and retreats down the stairs.

Their conversation doesn't last long, I hear my mother clambering up the stairs. I do not even look up to see her shocked face, I don't need to. I expect her to yell at me, to ask me what I have done. Instead, she says nothing, she just looks around at my mess of a room. At her mess of a daughter.

"You are a little old for that wallpaper anyways. What color would you like to paint your room? I always thought that it would look very pretty purple. What do you think?" She casually asks, as she circles my room picking up the destroyed wallpaper littering my floor.

"I like purple..." I mumble to her.

"You aren't going to yell at me?" I finally look up at her, and she is already turned towards me.

Her sigh is audible, "No, I am not, Ella. You are hurting, and I would never want to add your pain. Plus, I started hating that wallpaper a while ago." She lightens her tone with her last sentence. I do not know what to say, I am all cried out. I wonder what Reese said to her.

She clears me in, "So, Reese said that you didn't pick him up from school today. Eric dropped him off. Did you go to your appointment?"

"Yes."

"Did it help?"

"It did, but I won't be going again." It did, just not in the way that she had hoped. It was not a lie.

She looks as if she would like to argue, but stops herself. "Okay. Lets go buy some paint."

Chapter 9

"Ladies, we have been selected to participate in the championships!" My coach bellows at us in this emergency team meeting. Great. Now we have to practice more. I thought our last game was over with. What once seemed like such an honor, now seems like such a task. Everything feels like a task these days.

"Awesome! When is it?" Samantha questions him.

"Two weeks from today." Coach Briggs answers happily. "And, we are going to practice everyday after school until then! This is an honor ladies, and we need to make the most of it. If we win this game, we will get the championship trophy. We have not been chosen for this in years, we need to practice practice practice!"

Everyone is ecstatic. My teammates are going crazy. But me? I just want this year to be over. I want to graduate and leave everyone behind, this is just postponing time to myself.

"Ella, aren't you excited?!" Emily screams at me. Literally screams.

"Oh, yes." I sigh back.

"Come on El, you need to get out of this funk. We only have couple months left, let's make the most of it!" Samantha attempts to defuse my mood. It is not possible, everyday that I have to walk past Byron's locker is enough to make me go insane.

"Okay, okay I am sorry." Lie. Another lie.

"That is what I want to hear!" Tara joins in. "I am so sick of you being such a Debbie Downer!"

I can't help but agree with her. "A Debbie Downer huh? I am sorry. I will try my best to participate a bit more. How is that?"

"Sounds good to me." My friends all say, almost at once.

I know that they would like me to be more myself, but it has only been a month and a half since I lost my best friend. Is that really all it has been? He died a week before winter break was over, and we have been in school for a little over a month now. Six weeks, that is all that it has been. It feels like he was just here yesterday.

"Hey! Who are you?" I ask the new boy in class. He has short, black hair and eyes that he keeps lowered, looking at his lap.

"Byron." He says.

"Oh, hey Byron! My name is Ella, come sit by me!" I take him by the arm and lead him to the desk next to mine. "Mrs. Weaver, can Byron sit next to me?" I ask the teacher. We are in 4th grade, we are 10 years old.

"Yes, of course, show him around too would you, Ella?" She doesn't even look up from her computer.

"Yes mam!" I am eager to show this new boy around, to make him my friend. This quiet boy with the shining black eyes that I can now see as he looks at me, bewildered by my enthusiasm. "You heard her, Byron, I am here to show you the ropes. So hang on!" I laugh at my own joke.

"Okay." He mumbles at his lap, his head down once more.

What is wrong with this boy? "Byron, want to play with my calculator? I just got a game on it!" I don't know what else to say, even then, I always word vomited around him, I wanted to show off.

His eyes light up for the first time since I introduced myself, "What game?"

That was the first time I knew that this boy would be my friend. He was so quiet, and shy. In the mass of children screaming, he was alone. He drew me to him. Our personalities mixing, but clashing at the same time. Soon thereafter we both joined band, and our friendship was solidified.

"What is your elective class gonna be?" I ask the new boy, Byron.

He looks up from his homework, and blushes, "Band. I really like the trumpet."

I laugh at this irony sent from the fates, and he crunches his face at me, thinking that I am making fun of him. I quickly speak before he moves from me, "No, I just think it is funny because I chose band for the trumpet too."

He looks at me, almost puzzled by my reaction, "You are weird." Is all he states.

I look at him, and laugh again. This time, he moves seats.

Just as he moves seats, the teacher announces, "Now it is time to choose your elective classes, children. If you would like to join Art, go to class 1. Band, class 2. Fitness, class 3. Now off you go."

We all quickly make our ways to the classrooms, Byron walking behind the crowd, the unseen new boy. I wait for him by the door, so he knows what room it is in. He comes up behind me, and ignores me, quietly finding a seat marked Trumpet Section. I follow him, loudly plopping in the seat right next to him.

His sigh is audible, so serious, even as a kid. Before he can move, the band instructor begins speaking.

"Now that everyone is in here, we can begin. Where you are sitting now, will be your assigned seats, so get comfortable with the person next to you..."

I turn and whisper to Byron, "Looks like you have to be my friend, so buckle up for the ride." He looks over at me, and rolls his eyes, smiling all way.

I try not to think of him. I am like a zombie, wandering the halls. Zac passes me by, but has nothing to say. Once so happy, with life so perfect, it is now drab and bland. I have no yearning for Zac, as I once did. I have no urge to go out and party with my friends. Life just drags on. I cannot lift myself from this depression I have been so deeply inserted in. This must be how Byron felt.

My every being is changed, I am a different person. A different person with different thoughts, and a different personality. Everyone can see it, they know that I am changed. A ghost of my former self, Byron's serious facade now forever mine.

The weeks go by. I practice, I hang out with my friends, I laugh, I smile. But it is all a rouche. A sad rouche that I put on for others to feel better about themselves. I see Jerry and Rick, they are the only ones who understand. They are sad too. They let life go on without them as well, because life can't go on, not when your best friend is missing.

I find familiarity with them, we talk about Byron. We talk about the good times and the bad. I do not let them know about my feelings for him, nor the last time we saw each other. The kiss we shared. Those are not for sharing, not even with people who may shed more light on this boy for me.

"Aren't you supposed to be at practice or something?" Jerry asks me, as he passes me the joint.

We are hanging out at Rick's house in town, his parents are never home, his room is the entire downstairs. It reminds me of Byron's room, they bring me back to him.

"Yeah, maybe. I didn't feel like going." I reply, taking a hit of the weed. I have smoked before, only twice though. This is my third time. I like the feeling it gives me, a detached sense of myself. I am much happier when I am high, no wonder Byron started smoking the months before his death.

"Aww, Ella the little rebel." Rick teases me, he reminds me so much of Byron. I feel bad for using their friendship to hold me in the past, but I think that is what they are doing too.

"Yep, me the little rebel. I cannot wait for this awful year to be over." I groan, then start giggling. "I think I am high." I giggle again, Rick and Jerry begin giggling as well.

"I think you are, and so is Jerry." Rick punches Jerry in the arm as Jerry is reaching for the bag of chips on the table.

"Got the munchies?" I can't stop laughing, I am kind of hungry too. "Give me some of those chips." I flop over my chair and reach for the bag, heaving loudly. Rick grabs it before either of us can reach it, and starts eating them.

"Rick! Give them to meeee!" Jerry pleads, jumping on Rick to grab the bag. I begin laughing, appreciating the little world down here we have created through the haze. At this moment, I feel happy. Even if this happiness will not last, I enjoy it for the brief time that it is here.

Then, I remember, it is a school night and I am supposed to be home after practice. Crap. I look to Jerry, "What time is it?"

He checks his watch, the only kid I know to still wear one. Jerry has always been more old fashion, always wearing bow ties and suspenders. He fits the part down to his watch and bowling cap he wears. "5:30. Why?"

"I am supposed to be home after practice, which is about now. I have got to go guys. See yah later!"

"Bye!" They both yell to me as I run up the stairs to my car. I hear them then continue their arguing about the chips. That is another nice thing about Jerry and Rick. They don't question me, or make me act any differently than whom I have become. They live in the moment, a place that has become my home.

When I get home, my parents greet me and I excuse myself to my room. The phone rings, I do not answer. I do not care if it is for me, or not. I am too stoned to care about much right now.

"ELLA! PHONE!" Reese yells up the stairs. I sigh, and pick up the other line.

"Okay, I have got it." I say into the phone.

"Next time have them call on your cell, Ella. I was online." Click.

I chuckle, we still have slow speed internet. The new high speed internet is not yet offered in the middle of nowhere.

"Hello?" I ask.

"Ella! Where were you?" Emily sounds angry on the other line. "I tried calling your cell, but you haven't answered that thing in weeks. You missed another practice today."

She wants me to care about the game. When is it anyways?

"When is the game?"

"The game is in TWO FREAKIN DAYS, Ella. We need our point guard to come to practice. Do you know who has been filling in for you? A junior! A JUNIOR, Ella. She knows nothing."

"I am sorry, I guess I just spaced. I will be there tomorrow."

Her sigh is audible through the line, "Fine, Ella. But, please think of others. You are letting us down, just know that. And, you are letting me down. You may have lost one best friend, but you didn't lose your others."

Click.*

She hung up on me. She actually hung up on me. Emily is rarely angry with me.

She is right though. Byron may be gone, but Emily is still here. Tara is still here. Samantha. I have locked them out, not letting them help me. I have not been helping them, they knew Byron also. They grew up with him, he hung out with me and them.

Suddenly, my high is gone, and I feel rotten. Everyone is worrying about me. I am just as selfish as Byron. My self-loathing is like bile in my stomach. I feel sick. I need to let my friends know that I care about them. How quickly my happiness leaves me when it has the chance to run. I lay down on my bed, choosing to shut off my thinking, and wait for my parents to call for dinner.

I show up at practice the next day. All eyes are on me. Samantha bounds up to me first, "Feeling better, Ella? Coach has been worried about you, can't have you being sick for the game!" She winks at me, so I know that they have been lying for me to keep me out of trouble with the team. Even when I do not have their backs, they still have mine.

"Thanks Sam, I am feeling much better! Quite the stomach bug."

"Ella! Nice to see you are feeling better, I was worried that you wouldn't make it for our last practice before the game! Can't be having our best point guard down for the count." Coach Briggs comes towards me, a giant smile on his face.

"Yeah, Ella, glad you are feeling better." Jenny says, the junior who was to take my place according to Emily. I can tell that she is not as sincere as Sam and Coach.

"Thanks, everybody ready for some practice?" I shout at everyone, taking back my leadership in front of the team. Letting them know that I am back, I hear their cries in response. Everyones but Emily's, she will not look at me.

Practices goes by quickly, exercising is a natural high for me. We go over our plays, and plan for the game taking place the next day. My shallow breathing from the running allows my thoughts of agony to retreat back into my mind as I play the sport that I always have. It comes naturally to me, the only thing that has felt right in weeks.

"Alright, practice over! Showers ladies!" Coach roars at us, such a loud man. I am panicked and relieved at the same time that my time with everyone is over. The girls hustle over to the locker room, pushing each other and laughing. I gaze at them, but instead, I choose to go over and grab a ball. Practice is not over for me yet, I have some catching up to do.

"Ella, practice is over. Come on, let's go hang out or something." Tara tries to usher me to them, I shake my head at her.

"Nah, I think I need a little more practice before the game." She shrugs, having already given up with the others, and leaves me in the emptiness of the gym. Coach Briggs already out the door, probably off to his home like the others.

I hear the faint clanks of locker doors and footsteps retreating out of the building, I am alone. I begin working on my free throws, just concentrating on the hoop. The key to having a good free throw shot is to have a routine. Dribble, dribble, spin, dribble, dribble. Aim, shoot. The ball rolls off of my fingers, perfect arch, and a swoosh. It is all net, just like I knew it would be. Basketball is really just about practice, and repeat.

It is funny how such little things can now bring forth my happiness. I jog to retrieve the ball. Dribble, dribble. I spin the ball in my hands. Dribble, dribble. I keep my feet on the ground, bend, and shoot. Swoosh, goes the net. My free throw shots have always been my best. I smile at the net, shooting makes me happy.

My extended practice goes on, I lose track of time. All that I concentrate on is the ball and the net. I go in for the 3 pointer, it bounces off of the rim, a miss. The loud clanging of the hoop awakens me, I run to the ball now rolling towards the door.

A silhouette appears. He bends and picks up the ball before it rolls out the door. It is Zac. Of course it is.

"Thanks, Zac." I say to him as he tosses the ball back to me.

"You are welcome, Ella." He replies.

Our eyes lock. I miss him. But leaning on him to ease my pain feels like the easy way out, though it hurts us. I want to run to him, and wrap my arms around him. Being strong is so hard.

"I miss you." He says to me.

"How did you know I was here?" I ask, staying strong.

He spins the ball on his finger, staring at it, "I was coming here to practice, the janitor usually lets me in. Then, I saw your car." He drops the ball, and repeats his previous words, "I miss you, Ella."

I do not know what to say, my words fail me. I miss him too. I don't know what to do, so I walk over to him and fall into his arms, taking the easy way out. He holds me tight, I breathe in the scent of him. He smells like sweat mingled with his usual musky smell. He smells like Zac... I begin to cry. I haven't cried in front of anyone since my room incident. I hate crying in front of people. Seeing Zac here, alone, I am vulnerable.

My pain is almost palpable, I can't hold it in anymore. His touch rips me apart, seam by seam. It isn't the painful sobs either, it is a slow trickle of tears, my breathing uneven. I am not sure if I am sad or happy in his arms, I am too confused. Right now though, I honestly don't care.

Zac says nothing as I cry, he simply holds me. I do not deserve such kindness, I am a terrible person.

Eventually, I break away. "I am sorry, Zac. I am a terrible person, you don't want me."

Basketball gone from my mind, from his mind. Our thoughts are now only on each other.

He tilts my chin up, "Oh, but I do. You are strong, Ella. I know that, you have nothing to prove to me. I just want you to know that you can lean on me."

"Oh, Zac..." I kiss him. I can't help it, I need love. I need it to survive, it holds me up when I am falling down. I need him, and he will give me what I need. I slide my hand up to his chest, and press my body to his. I want to be with him. I can feel his heartbeat quickening, he wants me too.

"Is your mom home?" I know that there is usually no one at his house until late, when his mom gets off of work.

"No. Would you like to go there?" He asks me.

"Yes. Let's go, I want to be alone with you." And, that is all it takes.

Good thing his house is only minutes from the school, before I have time to change my mind. He takes me to his room, I have never been in his room. His mom does not allow us to be in there together, but I have never been here when his mom is not home. I think back to the first time I met Zac's family. It was Christmas break, days before Byron took his life.

"What if she doesn't like me?" I ask him, as he holds my hand, walking me to his front porch.

"She will love you, She has been wanting to meet you." He smiles at me. "Trust me."

He opens his door for me, and ushers me inside. He takes off my coat, and shows me to the dining room where we are having dinner. His house is large, but empty. The table is heavy with the food his mom has ready for me, she stands across the room, looking at me.

She is tall, rail thin, and intimidating, her hair is black and straight, pulled tightly from her face into a ponytail. Her dark eyes are serious, and she is holding a glass of red wine. His mom is gorgeous, and scary as hell.

She reaches her hand out to me, "Ella, I have heard so much about you. My name is Diane." I try not to stare, and reach out to shake her hand.

She then pulls me into a hug, her hug is not as bony as I thought it would be, it is a typical warm mother's hug. She lets go and continues, "I made us a traditional italian meal tonight! Show you our Italian roots, I will go get Zac's little sister and we can begin!"

She wanders off to get the little sister, whom I will soon meet, her name is Lilly. She is eight, and adorable. She will grow to love me in this short dinner date. As, Zac turns to me, he says, "see, she already loves you." And, I smile back, the night will go beautifully and I will fall in love with Zac for the first time, forgetting about Byron.

I wipe away the memory, forcing it into the back of my mind. I do not want to remember a moment where my heart betrayed my best friend. Maybe he knew, he could sense that I was ready to let him go. This is why I could not face Zac. The feelings intertwined, leaving me with fear and guilt. I shake my head, none of that right now.

Zac's walls in his room are painted a light blue. He has a twin size bed with navy blue sheets encompassing it. His shelf is oak, and holds action figures of every kind. I expected that. DVD's line another shelf with a small box tv above it. His dresser is clean, nothing is on it expect a couple photos. One of them being the one my father took of us before the dance.

I walk over, and pick it up. We look so happy. I look so happy... I run my finger along my face, so much has changed in the last two months. I look up, Zac is gazing at me. Waiting for my reaction. I walk over to him, and wrap my body around his.

"Are you sure you want to do this?" He asks me, genuinely concerned. He knows that I am a virgin, I know that he is not. I do not care. I need this.

"Yes." And when my mouth meets his, no more talking is necessary.

"Ella, I love you." I am wrapped in Zac's arms, our naked bodies intertwined.

"I love you too." I say, and I mean it. It is for even just a moment, the day when I fell in love with him. When I forgot about Byron.

He just took my virginity. The rest of my innocence is gone. Not a part of me remains untouched, my heart and soul. This is what I needed. It feels right, that in a time where I need love, I lose myself to it. It helps to soothe me. I am growing up. Though, I am not quite ready, I can ease my way into this life I have yet to begun to create for myself.

We lay there for hours, just cherishing each other's company.

Chapter 10

The game is over. Championships is done with. We lost. No, we didn't just lose, we were decimated. The championship team was from a much larger school than ours, we did not stand a chance. That is okay though, it was hard, but it was a good way to end the season. Going out, all the way, no matter the outcome.

Zac came to watch me, as did my parents and siblings. My grandfather even came out for the event. They cheered me on, and told me what a wonderful job I did after the game even though we lost. My family left me to Zac much quicker than they ever did in the past, I suppose having a depressed daughter who lost her best friend will give you a little leeway. Funny how that works.

"You did good, Ella. A good way to end the season, even if you lost." He is smiling at me, he means what he says. He always means what he says.

"Hey Ella, wanna go out with us tonight? We are going to have a movie night at Taras!" Samantha comes through Zac and I's conversation. Also all fired up from the game.

"Umm, maybe." I reply.

"Come on, El. You can bring Zac! It would be great to have you with us again. We keep missing you! And we can celebrate the end of the basketball season." Tara moans at me, showing up behind Samantha. Only Emily does not appear. She must still be angry with me… I have not talked to her since our fight the other day.

"That does sound like fun…" Zac says to me. Sam must have already told him about it. He seems quite for it, unusual for him. He looks innocently at me as I glare at him.

"Okay, I will be there." I say.

"Great! Hurry home now, and I will see you both at 8 pm sharp!" Samantha smiles at us, and walks away with Tara following behind her. I turn to look at Zac.

"Something tells me that you already knew about this movie night." I cross my arms at him as he hugs me loosely with one arm.

"Oh Ellie, you are too smart for you own good. I am going to head home to wash up, see you at 8?" His smile lights up his face, his charm warming my soul.

"Okay, I will see you at 8." I smile back, my shine still not reaching my eyes. That light will be gone a while. Zac turns and escorts me to my car.

I drive home, blaring the radio, it is playing Taylor Swift. She is light hearted, yet depressing at the same time. It fits my mood.

Life is trying so hard to capture me in its whirlwinds once more. It doesn't want me to stand still as it keeps going. I am getting catapulted back into this shithole called life. No, not shithole. That is harsh. Death is the shithole and I have been putting one foot in both. Life and death. Just hanging out in the middle, pretending neither existed.

I shake my head, I do not even know who I am anymore. Not quite alive, but not quite dead. No longer a child, but not quite an adult. This is too much. My feelings are so contradicting.

I pull into my driveway, Taylor Swift still screaming in my head. Time to enter my moment once more and get ready for this movie night… At least my parents will be happy that I am going out.

"Who is ready for some popcorn and pizza?!" Tara yells at us, as we are all getting settled into her den downstairs. It is her parent's designated spot for Tara and her friends. My friends are all basement dwellers.

Zac is sitting next to me, Emily is here with Ryan, Samantha, Colin, and Nate. Our little friend group combined with our boyfriends.

The only person missing would be Byron. He would have been invited, simply because I would have asked him to come. He would not have wanted to come knowing it would be all couples, he always felt uncomfortable around them. My awkward Byron… I can't help but to think of him, this is why I have been avoiding my friends, it hurts. The stabbing sensation that something is missing.

"Okay, okay. Horror movie first? I think yes." Colin is saying, as he looks through the movies that were rented.

"Ugh, I hate scary movies." Samantha moans, leaning further into the couch.

"Aww, don't worry babe, I will make sure to make it even scarier for you!" Colin teases her, as he slips in the dvd. As the sound starts in, I hear Tara banging down the stairs like a herd of elephants. How can one person make so much noise?

"Wait for me!" She squeals, and takes her seat next to Nate.

I like horror movies, the thrill and the scare that makes your heart beat faster. I also like that usually the dumb, loud people die first. To survive in a horror movie, you need to be strategic, and keep your wits about you. I would like to think that I would be the one to survive at the end of the movie.

Zac and I are sitting on the loveseat, Tara and Nate are squashed into an armchair, while the others are crowded into each other on the couch. Nate gets up to shut off the lights, I wonder what horror movie it is? The screen lights up, and I see the title invade the screen in bright green letters, FRIDAY THE 13TH. Great a gory movie. I feel Zac take my hand and I smile to myself. He thinks a movie like this could scare me when my life itself is a horror film. We settle in for the movie.

"Well, that was quite a movie wasn't it?" Zac says to me as the credits are rolling. Quite a movie? It was a downright gross movie. I release my hand from Zac's, two hours of movie time having cramped it up.

"Who thought it would be a good idea to remake Friday the 13th?" Emily replies from her spot on the couch between Samantha and Ryan. I laugh, and she glares in my direction. Then laughs with me, her grudges never hold. My random laughs, always the mood lightener, no matter the situation.

"I for one liked it, yeah it was gross, but for a horror movie? Not bad!" I chime in.

"You don't count, El, everyone knows you love a good murder flick." Emily points at me, and pretends to slit her throat falling dead on the coach. Everyone begins laughing, and mocking the movie.

"I bet the pizza is done by now, anyone want some" Tara asks, but she already knows the answer as we all run up the stairs. I am starving, and tonight, life feels normal again.

Soon, everyone is devouring the pizza, four pizzas may not be enough for the stomachs of the youth. Tara gets in the cupboard, retrieving chips and snacks to make up for the lack of pizza. Our conversation is halted as we eat, and it is nice.

Then the conversation turns to prom, I had almost forgotten it was coming up.

"So, everyone ready for prom?" Samantha asks everyone.

"Sure am!" Tara squeals.

"I have even picked out my dress." Emily states, proud of herself. She always gets things done with plenty of time in advance.

Then, all eyes turn to me, "What about you, Ella? You know, prom is only a couple of weeks away..." Emily says, trying to warn me if I had not remembered when it was.

"Umm, yeah, prom. It will be fun." I say, awkwardly, as Zac avoids my eyes, not knowing his place in my prom planning.

My friends seem to sense that this may be the end of the conversation, so they change the subject.

"What movie do you guys want to watch next?" Tara chimes on, pretending that the awkwardness never existed. But, it is too late.

Prom is on the table, and now I have to think about what I should do.

Tara asks me if I would like to spend the night with them when the boys go home. I say no, I am tired. Socially interacting after weeks of staying shut in my room is quite draining. I don't tell her that though of course, I just tell her that I am tired and want to sleep in my own bed tonight. She acts as if she understands, and so does everyone else, but they don't. I can see it in their facial expressions, that something is not the same about me anymore. I am not the person that I used to be, I do not fit in like I thought I always would.

Zac walks me to my door. "We should do this more often, Ella. Drive safe."
We kiss, a dry goodbye kiss. The passion swept under the rug from the night
before. He is taking baby steps with me, allowing me to lead.

He lingers, his words wanting to explode as mine does. It finally wins over,
I was expecting this. He looks down at me, "Ella, do you want to go to prom
with me? If you don't want to, I understand. I want to make the night special
for you."

He is blushing, this was hard for him. He needs my reply, and I need to
give it to him. I told myself that I would stop making others miserable, they
do not need to be miserable with me. Zac loves me, and my broken heart loves
him with all of its little pieces. I take a deep breath, pushing aside my miserable
being.

I smile, "I would love to go with you Zac."

It feels so normal, to say yes. His eyes light up my soul. I have made him so
happy, I can see it. His happiness spreads into me, I am happy that he is happy.
Love is finding its way back into my life.

He kisses me passionately, and tells me to call him when I know the color of
my dress. I nod my head, going with the conversation. He kisses me once more,
and we say our goodbye for the night. I clamber into my vehicle, and take the
back roads home.

Driving gives me a peace of mind. Tonight was normal, to the point of happiness. I enjoyed myself, but it felt fake, hollow almost. I know that I should be
attempting to get on with my life, but how are you supposed to go on with your
life when someone you love so deeply dies. Not just dies, but kills himself. My
friends do not feel the same guilt as me, because they were not as close to him.
They missed the signs because they did not know him, I knew him and let him
fade away.

I attempt to shake these thoughts from my head after such a great night. I
have great friends, a boyfriend who loves me and just asked me to prom, plus I
am going to graduate high school in less than two months. I should be ecstatic,
but instead, my guts clench as I think of the future. A future with one less person who made this world a bit brighter. How do people live through this pain?

Why am I letting this pain conquer my love and happiness? I am being torn in two directions, is this what depression feels like? Maybe as God's punishment for my negligence, he is forcing me to feel as Byron did. Some sick cosmic joke. I am not sure if I believe in God, but I do not like this God that has done this to me.

Home too soon.

As soon as I enter the door, my mother happily approaches me. "How was Tara's movie night? Did you have fun?" She tries not to sound too eager that I was hanging out with my friends again, but I can hear it anyway.

I plaster that smile upon my face, and reply, "It was great, we had a lot of fun. I am glad that I went out." I try so hard back, that my face is pinching, but she does not see it.

"Great! I am so glad. Also, how are those college applications going? You know that you graduate soon, I hope you are ready!" She smiles at me, assuming that I have already been filling them out, excited for my future. Instead I change the subject.

"Zac asked me to prom." I use the get out free card.

"Oh yay! I am so glad that you have decided to go, we can go pick out your dress next weekend!" She instantly changes from responsible mom about to lecture her daughter to I am so excited for my daughter's senior prom mom. I knew that would get her.

I let her babble on, and then I excuse myself to my room. Tonight was exhausting, she understands, her motherly concern and excitement allowing her to forget about my applications for another night.

I should start with the applications. I know this. I just do not know what I want to do, or where I want to go. There are so many options, so many different choices to pick from. It makes my head spin, I want to stay here. School is so simple, I have no worries, except the ones I create on my own. I try to understand the fear that was going on in Byron's head as he made his final choice, he cut off his path. He chose one, where no other possibilities could branch from it. I am afraid, but fear is what drives me.

My fear drives me to take different paths, I could never settle for one that breaks off so suddenly. I have been alone with my thoughts so much more than

I have in my four years of high school. It has given me so much to think about, what am I going to do with my life? I cannot settle into this place, I need to leave it behind.

I pick up my laptop and begin filling out an application that I have left blank on my screen for months.

I ignore Zac the rest of the weekend, and I hide from him in the halls the rest of the week until he hunts me down Friday as I am leaving school. I cannot face him, whenever I see him, normal life seems possible. I do not want normal life, I enjoy my isolation. He makes me too happy, he allows me to forget that Byron is gone.

"Ella, wait up! I want to talk!" He is breathless as he reaches me, I was almost to my car. What would I have done if I had gotten to it before him? Driven away like an asshole? Probably not, but it was a nice thought. I cannot handle confrontations, especially when I am not quite sure of my actions that lead to it.

I turn to him, "Yeah?"

"Ummm, you have been avoiding me… I just wanted to know what's up?" His gaze is filled with an underlying anger I immediately pick up on. Of course, he is angry with me. I am a jerk. I chase away my own happiness, this is my fault.

"I have no excuse, no reasoning. I just can't figure any of this out anymore. I need to be alone…" It is a sorry excuse of an excuse, I was better off mute, but it is all I have. After a week of pondering, I still don't know why I am doing this. To him. To myself. I do love him, but I feel incapable of love, I do not deserve it. I am too broken for normalcy, I must take God's punishment.

"You know what, Ella? Fine. Be alone. I am done." His venom paralyzes me, he is pissed.

I deserve it, I know that. Who sleeps with someone, and then freezes them out like that? I am a monster. I can only stare at him as he walks away, I have no more tears left.

What about prom I want to ask, but I have no right to ask that. I chose this unhappy path for myself, and now it is mine alone. What is wrong with me?

"Damn. You are cold." Reese sneaks up on me, he must have witnessed the whole thing. I see the worry in my sibling's eyes, I brush him off. I ignore him, and get into the car. This year cannot end soon enough.

Chapter 11

*T*rack season is here, my parents insisted that I participate like I have the
years before. Now, that I am on it though, I do not regret it. I forgot the
exhilaration that comes from racing. The wind whipping your face, stinging
your eyes, the muscles in your legs pushing to go faster, faster.

When I first started running long distance at 15, I had to have an inhaler.
I had been diagnosed with chronic bronchitis, making it hard for me to breath
after running at such a fast pace. I hate using my inhaler, so I switched to sprint-
ing. Therefore it did not affect me during basketball or track. The wheezing in
my chest just a constant reminder of my frailty.

I now run sprint races, and I pole vault, I have gone to the State championships every year in pole vault. This year I plan on breaking the school's record,
I am so close. This sport is the best thing for my happiness, it lets me feel free,
and I rarely think of Byron during it. Byron hated track, I remember our freshman year when I got him to join.

*"Pleaaase??" I begged him, "all of my friends are choosing softball, and I do not want to be
the only freshman to join!" I was on the point of shaking him until he said yes.*

*"Ella, your puppy eyes are not going to work. You know I hate running!" He was get-
ting exasperated, which means that I had almost won.*

*"Come on. If you do not like it, then you can just quit! Just try it, come on. I won't
ask you to do anything ever again." I am getting desperate. Tara, Samantha, and Emily
all chose Softball over track. I had no one, and that was not okay.*

*Byron rolls his eyes at me, letting my know that he does not believe I will stop asking
for things. "Fine, I will try it." I giggled in glee, I had won.*

Byron had not lasted a week, but by that time I was already so obsessed that I did not mind when he quit. He agreed to come to my home track meets to cheer me on, as long as he did not have to run anymore. We had agreed.

I shake the memories from my head, track has been going for a month now. I had run the majority of my races, and come in the top three every meet in my pole vault. I was on fire, sadness is quite the drive for success in this sport. It is hard to believe that in a month I will be graduating, and in less than that I will in the State finals for pole vault. My time was winding down, and I craved it.

The only downfall to track is that Zac is also in it. He hasn't even looked at me since we started practice. We pass each other by as if we never knew each other, and it hurts me to see us this way. I know that I only have myself to blame, but I cannot bring myself to approach him to apologize. The wounds are still too fresh. I cannot drag him into my abyss.

"Ella, may I please speak with you?" The principal approaches me. Her name is Ms. Plots, she is new this year, and I have barely spoken with her. I mean there has never been a point since I am leaving here soon.

I am almost too startled to speak, "Well, I am about to head to track practice but sure." She leads me to her office where I take a seat.

Her aged but still attractive face looks pained, as if she does not want to speak, "Ella, your grades have been falling." She says it as if I do not know.

I say nothing, and she goes on, "Since you have had perfect grades for the past year we have chosen to overlook this… umm, considering the past couple of months have been hard on all of us. But, another student has passed you in the running, so you are officially the Salutatorian of your class. That is still a high honor, I want you to know. You just need to keep your grades stable until graduation."

She tells me this as if I should be happy that I am still Salutatorian. Well, I am not. Byron was supposed to be my co-valedictorian, I did not want to be it without him. So, being at the top of my class is just the shell of who I used to be.

She looks at me, waiting for me to say something. I decide to give her a break. "That is great, I will keep my grades steady. Anything else?"

"Umm, no, just write your speech and finish your graduation duties. Thank you for your time." She stammers out the rest, not sure how to take my response. I know that I sound like Jack Frost, but I do not care, she interrupted my only peace.

I get up from my chair and exit. Practice is already underway. I jog to make the rest of practice, the only place where my thoughts will not overcome me.

"Hey Mom, Dad. I thought I would let you know that I am officially Salutatorian." I smile at them. We are sitting around the dining room table, our now mandatory family dinners since my behavior after Byron's death.

"Congratulations honey!" They both say, choosing not to ponder aloud why I have fallen to second.

"Way to be the smart one." Reese jokes with me, letting me know that he is also proud of me.

Our bond has deepened since the night he held me in his arms as I cried in my mess of a room. We appreciate each other more, and understand each other, he respects me and I him. I also think he is afraid to lose me, everyone walks on tiptoes around me.

"Thanks, Reese." I smile at him, I am happy that my family is proud of me.

"Well, I guess we better start planning your graduation party! Any ideas on it yet?" My Dad asks me.

"Actually yes. I would like to have a memorial for Byron at my graduation, and allow his family to set up a place for him alongside my achievements. Is that okay?" I ask them.

I have thought about this quite a bit, and we were going to have our graduations together. This way, I can still include him in my happiness. I can see my parents sharing a look, but they say nothing except that it sounds wonderful.

"Have you thought about your graduation party yet?" I ask Byron, as we sit in his room downstairs. Our homework sprawled all over his desk, and cheetos staining his book from my orange fingers. He picks up his book, and attempts to clean the crumbs from it.

"Kind of, but not really. I am assuming you have?" He knows me so well. Of course I have.

"Yep! Emily and Tara are having their parties together, and Samantha doesn't want to share her party. Since, it is a day all about her." I chuckle. "But, I was thinking since our brothers had it together, we could have it together too! I mean our parents already have everything for it. Whatcha think?" I want him to say yes.

"Hmmm, will your dad be cooking?" My dad is a grill master.

"Of course!"

Byron's eyes twinkle, "Then, I guess we can. As long as you plan most of it."

"Anything to get out of some extra effort huh bestie?" I jab him in his side, making him laugh at me and look up from the paper he was scribbling equations all over.

"Hey, I am agreeing aren't I?" He is right, he went down without a fight at all. I should be thankful.

"You did, don't you worry. I have got this!" I sashay my way to his desk, and pretend that I am a prima donna. He shoves me off, shaking his head at me.

"I bet you do." He replies.

School. Practice. Homework. Sleep. Repeat. That is how my days wear on, and on. I think that prom is this weekend, but I have forgotten. My mother and I did go out to get a dress, she was too excited for it that I did not tell her that I had ruined it like normal. So we got a dress, a gorgeous long black dress. It was sleek, and held my curves in in all the right ways. The best part, was how it sparkled like the night sky. It reminded me of Byron, I liked to think of him as a star shining in the sky. My beautiful star that had fallen from the sky, overcome by the darkness. My forever falling star.

My mother had said it was very adult, and made me look beautiful. It was not the normal dress I would have chosen only months before. I had liked princess dresses and bright colors. My taste changed with the passing time, the passing of my childhood.

I have not yet told my mom that I would not be going, I know that she will have a fit. So, I bought my ticket to show her, to ease her worries about not having seen Zac around. Maybe, I will go. Just to pass the time, and the dress does look good on me. But the idea of seeing Zac there with someone else just hurts. I don't know.

The school days pass by in a blur, my head in the clouds, or better, beneath the ground. I finally have the weekend, no track meets or time required to spend with my friends.

"Ella, you have a letter for you!" My mom yells up the stairs. A letter for me? I wonder from who?

I rush down the stairs, grabbing it from my mother's hands, she laughs at me. I have never gotten a letter before, I flip it over in my hands. It is a small manilla envelope, tattered but intact. It has no return address on it, addressed to me, Ella Cane. I study it a moment longer before opening it, then realizing, that handwriting. I would know that sloppy writing anywhere.

I waste no more time, and tear it open.

Oh. My. God.

It is from Byron. Maybe this is a giant hoax, and he is alive elsewhere? Hope raises in my chest, then reality turns it to bile. No, I cannot raise false hope before reading this. Byron is dead. How did he? I begin to read;

Hey Elly Belly,

You are probably wondering a lot of things right now. But, no, I am not alive somewhere else. If you are reading this, it means that I went through with it. I am dead. It means that I gave this to the post office, and asked them to wait to mail it. I wanted you to get it after the pain of my absence has hopefully faded a little, and you are almost done with our Senior Year.

I want you to know that I chose this. I chose it because I am miserable in life. I am not sure if I can be here anymore. I want you to know that this was not anyone's fault but my own. I am sorry that I cannot be strong, I am weak, and selfish. You probably hate me, I know that. I would rather have you hate me, if it makes it easier for you.

So, here it goes. Please don't blame yourself for this, or feel guilty (I know you are, so stop it). I want you to get out of this town, and do whatever you want with you life. You are perfect, Ella. And, you don't need me around holding you back, or anyone at all.

I am writing this the night we kissed. Oh Ella, you sent me for a spin. Kissing you was something I never thought I would get. And, I am sure you understand why I could not love you how you needed me to now. But, I want you to know that I do love you. I love you, Ella Cane. I loved you, and you showed me happiness when the darkness pulled me lower everyday.

I am sorry that I left you, but the hole kept sucking me in, and I could not stop it. So, I guess, what I have left to say is, move on. Forget about me, and keep that charm of yours. Dream big, Ella.

Love,

Byron

Oh, Byron. I clutch the letter close to me, and sob. I sob, and sob. I choke my face into my pillow, I do not want my family to hear. They want me to be okay so badly, but I am not. He loved me. He fucking loved me, and he still left. He left me. I want to hate him so much, hating him is so much easier. He wants me to go on like nothing ever happened? What a selfish, gaaah.

I can't hold the pieces together anymore, I am breaking. My sobbing and thoughts jumble together, they are me. I am a mass of pain, I choke my face farther into my pillow. I scream, and scream. I need to get out of here. I blindly reach for my shoes, I will go for a run.

I run out the door, tear streaked, telling my mother I needed to go for a run. I did not give her a chance to respond. I am breaking apart at the seams. My feet hit the dirt, and I run.

I turn off my brain, as the tears still run down my face. It is dusk, the chill settling in from spring. We live on a dirt road back in the country, I can run the entire block, it is only six miles. I make the turn to loop around, my tennis shoes smacking the dirt, leaving a cloud in my wake.

How could he write that to me? How could he say all those things like they even mattered now? He is dead. He is gone. Reading his words only allows me to revisit our memories. Memories. That is all they are now. My chest hurts, the cold and the heartbreak constricting my chest. I miss him so much, it hurts. He left me. I can't stop repeating it in my mind. Was he really that afraid of going on? He could have talked to someone, he could have been okay.

The memories begin exploding around my mind. He changed me, his absence is shaping who I am becoming. I hate that his death can change my very core. How dare he interrupt my life once again with his thoughts, his thoughts that will never be here again. I hate him. I hate him. I want to hate him.

I keep running, faster and faster. Thoughts flooding my already blurred vision. I want to die so much right now, to just be with him. The pain is unbearable.

I am almost onto what feels like my 5th mile. I am tired, but I do not want to stop. I almost there, I may not have been able to control my life, but I can control my running. I quicken my pace, I can feel my chest continuing to constrict. It helps me to forget the emotional pain, it lets me feel only the physical.

I am almost back home, I am so tired.

Here!

I stop, screeching to a halt in front of my house. I can't breathe, the pain is horrible. It is no longer emotional though, my breaths are coming out in wheezes. No, not right now. I stumble to the door, gasping for air, my mom reaches for me. My inhaler. The cold air. Not paying attention. Bad combo. The blackness is engulfing me. Maybe, I want to die. I embrace the dark.

I can barely move when I wake up in the hospital bed. They told me that I had an asthma attack. The cold mixed with the distance that I ran made it hard for my lungs to get in oxygen. Since my lungs are covered in mucus from the chronic bronchitis, I just shut down. I could have died they said.

I could have died. My mother is moaning from the side of my bed, they are going to keep me here over night. My eyelids feel so heavy, the drugs numb my body, I feel sluggish. I think I need to sleep. Why am I not dead? It would be so much easier to just die. I close my eyes once more.

I wake in halts over the course of the night, sometimes I hear the mumbled voices of my family, John is here too. He must have come to visit me from college. What a good brother...

"Ella, Ella?" Emily is standing over me. She looks tired, or maybe it is because she is wearing no makeup.

"Hey, Em..." I mumble at her, still registering my surroundings. Oh yeah, the hospital. I feel much better from yesterday.

"Oh my gosh, are you okay? Tara and Sam wanted to come but they would only let one of us in!" She is frantic, I must look bad. And, I thought she looked bad. Emily only acts frantic in extreme cases.

"I am fine, just pushed a little too hard." I think back to the letter. I chose to let the physical pain overtake me instead of thinking about what I really needed to.

Emily breathes a sigh of relief, "Everyone is so worried, when are you getting out?"

"Today, I think?" I had no idea.

"Okay, great! Prom is tomorrow night and you have to go." Emily states.

I laugh at her, "I feel like shit, and you are pestering me about prom tomorrow?"

"Yes mam, I like to keep it normal. We can even take you in a wheelchair if we must." She has that determined look on her face. I sigh, I am too tired to argue.

"Fine. You have to let me sleep then." I moan.

"Sounds good to me, here are some flowers. I will see you tomorrow. Rest up, Em!" She shoves the flowers in my arms and bolts.

That was weird. Maybe she doesn't like hospitals or something. Prom? Of all things, she is an evil genius, I am way too tired to argue.

I can't wait to get out of here, everyone fawning over me makes me feel uncomfortable. I mean, everyone has a little collapse every now and then, right? Sure, I was probably a bit hysterical, but I am fine now. I hope my parents don't overreact.

I wonder where they are right now. Probably out getting breakfast or something. I want to leave.

Soon, my family arrives, I smell Mcdonalds on their breaths. That sounds so good right now. They all pile in, and smile at me, like a bunch of hyenas surrounding my bed.

"Hey, Ella! Feeling better?" John is the first to speak to me.

"Yeah, I am fine. Do I get McDonalds?" My parents and brother laugh at my response, relieved by my bouncing back.

"No, not until we check you out. We will take you there or anywhere else that you want to go." My mother looks like she is about to cry with joy.

"Okay, great. Lets go."

My mother looks at me all worried, "Well you are not supposed to leave until tomorrow. You need to rest up, and let the doctors look at you."

I glare at them, "I want to go now."

"Sorry honey." My Dad says, stroking my arm. I choose another tactic, and turn to my mom.

"Mom, prom is tomorrow. You don't want me to miss it do you?" I give my best puppy dog eyes. I hate this hospital feeling, and I need to leave. I will even go to prom if it lets me get out of here.

"Oh Ellie, fine, let me go talk with the doctor and get your medicine and inhaler." My mom scurries away, hopefully I have won.

My brothers aren't sure whether to pat me on the back for my cunning tactic, or laugh. I see John chuckle.

"So, how about that Mcdonalds?" I ask again.

The ride back home is anything but relaxing as the doctor said my next few days should be, upon my discharge. My brothers are bickering on either side of me, crammed in with me since my parents did not think of the return with an extra person in the car. The entire car now smells of grease and fried food from our two stops at Mcdonalds, the boys wanting to eat again along with me.

My stomach is already churning from the drugs, the food, the smelly car, and the drive itself. They are lucky that I do not puke on them all.

Once we reach home, my parents send me straight to my room to rest for the rest of the day. Great. They say nothing else about my run the night before, not wanting to relive it again. They must not know why I was so upset, I reach into my night stand and pull out Byron's letter.

I stare it, reading it once more. It does not upset me as it did when I first read it. My breakdown is over, the rush to the hospital gasping for breath drained me enough. I almost died with Byron. He probably did not see that coming.

I think back, I had wanted to die. I pat my lungs, but they did not let me. I now have a hitch in my breath, but I am not dead. I don't think that I really wanted to die. Almost dying is better than dying because it gives you a chance to fight back.

I feel like someone new once more. I saw my family's fear at losing me, and I could never do what Byron did. I could never leave the people that love me. It is not my fault that he died, he is right. It was his own, he didn't think through his choices, and chose a permanent state for his temporary feelings. I have been so filled with sadness, that I have been letting the same black hole that dragged him down, tear me down as well. His emptiness became my own.

I almost died yesterday, but I was afraid. I have never known true fear until my own death was staring back at me. Byron says that he was afraid, afraid of growing up, afraid of future choices. He was frightened by the darkness that blinded him, he chose to end his life. Byron was selfish, and stupid, but in his death, at least his last moments were of courage. I try to comfort myself. His choices were his own.

Byron never had the chance to see the fear on his loved one's faces when they thought he might die. Maybe then, he would have changed his mind. Chosen to conquer his emotions and sadness. I understand now that I lost my best friend, and a piece of myself, but I did not lose myself. I still have a life to live, and choices to make. I have just been walking through these past few months in a daze that I was unable to shake.

He was right, his letter did help. I am going to start living again.

Prom is today. I slept all day yesterday, hoping to feel better. Emily has called, she will be picking me up in a couple of hours. I will be going stag, I wish that

I could call Zac to tell him how sorry I was, but my fear will not allow it. It is time to get ready, I still have trouble moving around for too long. My lungs need to take breaks, my mother sees me struggling but does not want to be the one to tell me that I cannot go to prom.

Emily arrives an hour ahead of time to help me finish getting ready, my mom must have called to tell her that I am struggling. Emily quietly helps me with my hair and makeup. Things have been different between us since Byron died. She knows that I am hiding something from her, but I am not ready to reveal it.

"There, all done." She smiles at me in the chair, and turns me to face the mirror. I look gorgeous, though a little pale from my attack. My hair is curled, and falling in tendrils around my face. My eyes are done a charcoal black to match the dress, and my lipstick is a deep red. I look hot.

I look up to face Emily, not wanting to cry. She looks beautiful as well, in her off white strapless princess dress. Her hair in a bun, she looks like a princess too.

"Thanks, Em. I look great, almost as beautiful as you." I smile at her, the smile finally beginning to reach my eyes.

She smiles back, unsure of my reaction. "Thanks, Ella. Now, lets head to prom shall we?"

We hook arms, and descend the stairs. My parents once again, insist on snapping pictures, but before they do. I hear the doorbell.

"Now who could that be?" Emily asks, wide eyed and guilty. I hear him, before I see him.

"Hello, Mr. Cane. Please to see you again." Zac is here. I freeze. Why is he here?

"Emily.." I say, turning to her.

"What? You told him yes, I figured I would just tell him it was still a yes." She laughs at my exasperated facial expression. "Hey! Now you have a date! Everyone else will be here in a minute. Now, isn't it time you begin enjoying yourself again?"

I want to cry. Again. I am such an emotional wreck, and crying would only make me wheeze and ruin my makeup. I turn to Zac, he looks right at me.

"Hey Ella, you look great. Ready for prom?" He smiles at me, his lopsided grin that I fell in love with. Maybe, I could fix things yet.

Everyone is arriving, Sam and Tara with their dates. Ryan shows up for Emily, everyone asks how I am and lets my parents know that they will be watching over me so that I do not overextend myself.

After pictures, and awkward smiles between Zac and I, we are out the door. I am not allowed to drive, so Zac takes me. The night seems almost like a deja vu of winter formal. Except, this time the prom is being held in a real ballroom. I can almost feel the excitement bubbling up in my chest, or maybe I just needed my inhaler.

The prom goes by in a whirlwind, I sit most of it out because I am still having trouble breathing, but Zac keeps me company. We do not talk about anything that could ruin the night, we only talk about the dance. I want to tell him so many things, but I am a coward. He is halting in his speech with me, like he is waiting for me to say something, but I do not.

"So, nice dance right?" I say.

"Yes, nice dance." He replies.

We do not even discuss my attack, he does not even ask about it. We are friends, nothing deeper. We are prom dates, but only for this night. So I decided to take advantage of it, of this pact we have formed.

"Want to dance?" I ask him.

"Can you?" He asks back, surprised.

"Only slow ones."

"Are you sure?"

"Yes."

"Okay."

He helps me stand, and we make our way to the dance floor. The song is slow and moving, it is a song for couples. Zac puts his hands on my waist, and I reach my arms up to his shoulders. I lay my head against his shoulder.

"Oh Zac…" I say.

"Shhh, nothing tonight." He says back, shutting me down before I can even begin. He tilts my head up to his, "nothing matters tonight but us." I look up at him, and he kisses me, hard. I am sick of this prom, I want to get out of here. It is suffocating me, all I want is to feel Zac's body against my own.

I go for it, "Want to get out of here?" I ask.

He looks down at me, "my mom isn't home." He blushes, and I blush back.

"Let's go."

We go hand in hand out the doors, saying goodbye to no one, our eyes only on each other. I am determined to make my life worth living again, and that means letting myself love again.

Chapter 12

oday is the State Championship for pole vault, I also qualified for the 200 meter dash. I am proud of myself, I did not think that I could get back into it after my attack.

Zac and I have not talked since prom TWO WEEKS AGO. He has been avoiding me, which I know I deserve. He is doing back to me what I did to him. I am in love with him, I finally know that. I just don't know what to do about it.

We stayed with each other all night, rediscovering each other's bodies.

"I want you." Zac says, unzipping the back of my dress. I moan as his hands find my hips, and move up to my breasts.

"You have always had me" I say. Allowing myself to be taken once more. No words were necessary. Nothing was said until we awoke in each other's arms in the early morning.

"I should leave." I say to him, getting dressed back into my gown, now feeling awkward. I need to get home before my parents wake up and discover me missing, or before Diane catches me here.

He watches me, and says nothing.

"Okay, so, see you later?" I say. I am a coward, I want to say more, but I don't.

"Okay." He finally says, and I wish that I could tell him what I want to say, need to say. But that would break the rules we had bestowed for the night. Does it carry over until morning?

"Okay." I say, and make my quick exit, hating myself the whole way back to my house.

Since then? It was like nothing had happened, we continue to pass each other by in the halls. Polite hellos, and head nods. Maybe this is what we need, a thinking period. I am glad Regionals, they are a welcome distraction to my racing thoughts.

I still can't wrap my head around that I actually made it to State after the year that I have had. Even with the week I had to take off following my attack, and how my coaches wouldn't let me race until they saw me practice for a week after that. They almost wouldn't let me compete at Regionals, we see who won that battle! I was so determined, practicing my vaulting every night after practice. The highest I have vaulted is 9'6'', school's record is 9'10''.

I can do this.

I know that I will not actually win at State; the girls there have been vaulting much higher than me. I have a chance of placing though, but all I want is that record. The 200 meter dash just requires me to run my fastest, not much in explaining that.

My parents and brothers are all going to be at the meet, along with my team coming to cheer me along. Zac also qualified for state. He qualified in the hurdles. Now we are on this bus together with only a couple others, and I badly want to talk to him...

He has frozen me out, like I did to him. We had reformed our friendship at prom, but nothing has come from it. I must mean nothing to him. Oh how I want to apologize. I need to tell him that I was an asshole, and that I know that I do not deserve his forgiveness for my actions, but I want him to know how sorry that I really am. This is my chance.

He is sitting on the seat behind me. I can hear his music playing in his headphones behind me. He is not asleep like the rest of the people, he must be nervous also. I turn around to face him.

I tap his shoulder, he looks up at me quizzically, and takes out an earbud, "Yeah?"

"Hey, wanna come up here and talk to me for a second?" I stammer out.

"No." He looks away from me, out the window, and puts his earbud back in.

Well, I guess I got my answer pretty quickly. I reach into my bag to pull out my Ipod for the rest of the trip, and then I feel my seat move. Zac plops down beside me, "Okay, let's talk." He says, and crosses his arms next to me.

I turn to face him, this is my chance. I can't look at him and say what I am about to say, "Zac... I am sorry for how I treated you, I had reason to cut you out like that, I am an asshole. You deserve an apology. You wanted to help me and I just pushed you away. I wanted to apologize at prom, after prom..." My gaze raises when I am done talking, and Zac's stare is piercing. Then, his expression softens as he looks at me, my face laid bare, open to his evaluation of my honesty.

"Oh, Ella. I was so worried when I heard about your hospital visit. I should have said something, but when I showed up to take you to prom, I did not know what to do." He says to me, not caring about my apologies.

"So, you forgive me?" I wonder aloud.

"Not entirely, but it is a start. I know what you did, Ella. I can see right through you, I just wanted to help, and you pushed me away. I was just hurt, but I understand that you needed time to yourself. I was afraid you would reject me at prom." He looks out the window, and exclaims, "Well, looks like we are there. Cheer me on today?" He smiles at me and slides back to his seat to grab his stuff.

"It's a deal." I say, smiling at myself.

It is going to take time to undo all the pain that I have caused others in my mourning of Byron and my own self pity. Zac loved me. Risked being rejected for prom, but still showed up at my house. I do not deserve his love, no wonder he needed time to think.

The bus comes to a stop, and our coaches usher us off. No pep talks in track, you get out there and motivate yourself, and if you do well, you get a pat on the back from a coach. Now I would like a medal and a pat on the back, that would make my day complete.

I grab my bag, and follow everyone off of the bus. My day is off to a good start, lets see if I can make it even better.

"Come on, Ella! You got this!" My family and friends cheer me on.

I am on my last vault, if I do not make this jump then I will only tie the school record, but if I make it... I will advance to the finals, and I will surpass the current record holder. This is my chance, I can do this.

I already ran my 200 meter dash, I did not even make it out of the preliminaries, the girls were just too fast. I have this now, ignoring the cramps that I have in my chest. Just one more good vault. I look out at the crowd, steadying my breathing.

I cheered on Zac as he made it to the finals in the hurdles, and I see him now as he cheers me on. My name is called, and I make my way to the runway, with my pole in hand. Why did I have to choose such a difficult event? Everyone is staring me down, the competition is fierce.

My breaths are coming in gasps, today has taken its toll on me, but I can do this. All I have to do is give it my all. I concentrate, and block everyone out. This is me. I begin my sprint down the runway towards my destination, the bar dangling almost 10'' in the air.

I ram my pole into the box, and lift myself into the air, lifting my feet above my body to throw myself over the bar. I slide over the bar, and throw my pole back behind me. I begin to flip my body forward over the bar, and land on the mat behind it. I am on my back staring at the bar as it begins to wobble, I must have nicked it on my way down. It continues to wobble, and I lay motionless, not wanting to tempt the fates, but they must have been tempted enough.

Seconds later the bar falls, the crowds exhales the breath they were holding. It is over, I am out. I may not have gotten the record all to myself, but at least I tied it. That is what I tell myself anyway. I grab my pole, and make my way over to my family, they try to hide the disappointment on their faces.

"That was so close, Ella!" My dad comforts me, wrapping his arms around my shoulders. My mom, and brothers join in.

"Yeah, that was a great vault!

"And you tied the record, that is great!"

I try to smile at them, but I am too exhausted and disappointed in myself. My dad asks me if I would like to leave with them, but I shake my head, I still have to watch Zac in the Finals. I need to redeem my actions over the last couple of months. They are ready to go, the sun has been beating down on everyone all day, the awakening of spring. I tell them that I will see them when I get home, and we part ways.

My coach waves at me from across the crowd, I see him motioning towards the track. Zac must have left for his Finals, I better not miss it. My own disappointment will not leak on to his chances, I find my way to the railing, and see him at the starting line getting ready.

"Good luck, Zac! Cream them!" I yell. He looks in my direction and smiles before getting back to his preparations. At least he knows that I am watching, I hear the countdown on the loudspeakers begin.

"RUNNERS, ON YOUR MARKS. GET SET. GO!" And the gun goes off.

It is dark by the time we all clamber back onto the bus, exhausted and hungry. The bus driver promises that we will stop at Taco Bell on our way back, we are all thankful, though I am sure she is hungry as well. It was a long day.

Zac placed 2nd in the final round of hurdles. I am so proud of him. And me? I missed my last vault. I tied the school record, and placed 6th overall.

As I crash into my seat, I swear I could almost fall asleep right here. The sun drained my energy, and vaulting has made my arms feel like Jell-o.

I can't help but feel a little bummed, I have been practicing so hard just to have my name on that board with another. This was my last chance. Not what I wanted, but with my karma, I am glad that I got that. Life never is fair, I should know that by now. I lean my head on the window, preparing for the long ride home.

Just as I am about to doze off, I feel that familiar flop of the seat next to me, I don't even have to turn to know who has joined me.

"Hey Zac, congrats on the 2nd place." I mumble to him, lifting my heavy eyelids from their sleepy state.

He nudges me, "Thanks, Ella. Congrats to you, tying the record isn't bad! You worked hard, even after your time off. You look a little tired."

I can't even lie to him, even though I do want to talk. I am still not as strong as I was before my hospital visit. "I am, today took a lot out of me."

My smile does not convince him, he knows that I am feeling weak.

"Well don't let me stop you from sleeping, I have been told that my chest is a great pillow. Just saying." He jokes with me, and after momentarily pausing, he puts his arm around me. There are so many things that I want to tell him, but instead, I lean into his chest and fade off into my dreams.

I must have slept right through Taco Bell, because the bus is arriving at the school when Zac wakes me.

"Oh wow, I slept through food?! Maaan…" I wine. Then I notice the bag that he has next to him, and he hands it to me. "For me?"

He laughs, "yep, you were just too cute to wake up, so I had the bus driver grab us some. Is that alright with you?"

I grab the bag, "That is fine with me." Then I hesitate. "Zac, why are you being so kind to me?" I want to pretend that everything can go back to normal, but school is almost over and I know that I hurt him.

Zac shrugs, "How about we make our way to your car and we can talk? I think the bus driver wants to head home." I look around, he is right, she is waiting on us. I nod my head, and we make our way to my car.

It is too cold to stand outside, so I slide into my drivers seat, and turn on the heat from the chilly night air. I motion for Zac to join me, he opens the passenger door, and for a moment we are both quiet.

"Ella, I still love you. That is why I am so nice to you, because I still want to be with you. I always have." Zac speaks quietly at first, and then grows more confident. "I don't care if you kissed Byron, I am glad you did because at least you had that moment before he was gone. I know you are in pain, and that for some stupid reason you are blaming yourself. I know you are, everyone can see it. But, people love you Ella, and everyone misses you."

How could he still love me? After everything. I froze him out, and then I lost my virginity to him, and froze him out again… I cheated on him with Byron, and I hurt him. I have hurt so many people in my own despair, but they miss me? No. They miss the person I used to be, and I cannot go back to her.

"Zac, I love you too. I always did, but, we are both graduating soon, how could this work? And, I am not the person you fell in love with anymore. People miss me, but I cannot go back to who I was. That person is gone, she died with Byron. I wish I could go back to who I was, but I can't. I am different, I can feel it. I cannot keep leading you on, I am a mess."

Zac looks as if he wants to interrupt, but I continue, "When I was in the hospital, the doctors told me that I almost died. I can't believe that, it almost was surreal to me, but death was never in my radar before Byron. It is like his death, woke me up to reality. Before, I didn't believe that anything could happen to me, and now? I know something can happen to me, but that isn't what scares me the most. What scares me the most is knowing that death can take away the people that I love. That they can disappear from my world forever."

There, I said what even my thoughts haven't spoken aloud. Zac only stares at me, and I stare back, urging the tears back. I don't want to love anymore, because when that love is gone, only a hole remains.

"Oh, Ella. You are so naive. Death is inevitable, but it is what makes life so valuable. You of all people, will never stop loving, you will never stop caring. You freezing me out? Freezing your friends out? That is proof that you are still the Ella we all know, and no amount of changing can take that part of you away. So push me away all you want, but sometimes you have to take the risk. Byron dying didn't make you love him any less, and pushing me away won't make me love you any less."

"Zac... I am so broken." I fall into his arms, as I attempt to push the tears away. I have cried more in the past couple of months than I have in years.

"I can't fix you, Ella, only you can do that. But, I will be here to help you pick up the pieces." He kisses my hair, and moves down to my forehead, making his way down to my nose, my cheeks, my chin, and finally he kisses my lips.

'You can't fix sadness', Byron's words echo in my head. But now I know that he was wrong. You can fix your life, you just need to try.

Zac pulls away before I lean in, craving more. "And, I am going to give you as much time as you need to find you. If you realize that you can't be with me, then I will accept that, but, I want you to think about it. If you want to be with me, then even different colleges won't keep me from you."

"Okay..." I whimper. I don't know what I want. My thoughts are still untangling when I notice him opening the door to exit.

"I will see you at school next week, Ella. I love you, have a good night." And he shuts the door.

I don't know what to think, how can he forgive me so easily for everything? This gives me hope, before I go home, I have one more person I need to see. One more broken piece of my life that I can fix.

I don't bother calling or texting before I show up, I know she will be home. I pull into the drive, and shut off my car. This is my chance to make things right. I walk up to her door, and knock.

I only wait a moment before I hear footsteps, and Emily opens the door.

"Hey Em..." I say.

For a moment she just gawks at me, then, she smiles, "Hey Ella, come on in."

I smile at her, and walk on in, shutting the door behind me.

I say hello to her parents, and we go right to her room. Her parents are used to friends randomly showing up, that is what it means to have a teenage daughter.

We get to her room, it is tidy as always with not an item out of place. Typical Emily. I sit down on the white comforter covering her bed, as she takes a seat at her desk across from me.

"So, what is up?" She asks me, no beating around the bush with her.

This is it, I take a deep breath, "Em, I am so sorry for the way I have been acting. I shouldn't have iced you out like that... Byron may be gone, but I still have a best friend, and I guess I forgot that."

She waits a moment before talking, "Ella, I was just mad that you blocked me out... It was like when Byron died, you died too. You forgot you had other friends who were hurting too, and who could have helped you. Like me. It was like I wasn't even your best friend anymore."

"I know, and you are my best friend! I just needed time to myself, seeing everyone just reminded me that Byron was missing. I felt like I couldn't continue on with daily life, knowing that he was gone... I shouldn't have pushed you away, I was just so lost."

I look down, and Emily reaches over to grab my hand, "I know you are lost. You loved him, everyone could see it. Your heart is broken and it hurts, but I only want to help. You can always talk to me, Ella. You were always so weird when you were around Byron, and none of us knew what to say to you when he died because we never knew your feelings about him."

"Emily, I loved him so much. I didn't want to tell you, the way I felt was just too personal to express." I try not to cry as I prepare to tell her the rest.

"Byron knew that I loved him, I told him about a month before he killed himself. I also kissed him the week before he died, and he told me I would understand later. He started stealing and smoking and acting out, I should have seen it! I let him down, and now I don't deserve another best friend because I will just let you down too."

Somehow I hold it all together, it must be my exhaustion from the meet. I am too tired to even cry, but I had to do this tonight. Emily doesn't even hesitate as she bursts into tears, and almost knocks me over with the force of her hug.

"Oh Ellie, I had no idea what you were going through! I am such a terrible best friend for being so mad at you! I should have seen you were in pain, none of this is your fault. None of it all, including Byron's death. I love you." She is crying on me, and suffocating me at the same time.

"Thank you for never giving up on me. I am glad we are good, now get off of me!" I jokingly retort (kind of), and push her off of me.

"Looks like my old best friend is starting to show herself a little bit." Emily laughs back at me, releasing me from her grip and moving to sit next to me, instead of on top of me.

I breathe freely for a moment, realizing that I really wasn't able to breathe as she was on me. It takes me more than a moment before I get my breath back. Emily notices, "I am sorry! I forgot you had a meet today, and your lungs problem." I wave off her concerns.

"It's fine, but I am really tired and need to head home. We can talk more tomorrow?" I ask her hopefully.

She nods ferociously at me, "of course! Go home, I will definitely come over. We have a lot to talk about." With that, she walks me to the door.

"Ella, I am really glad you came over."

"Me too." I say smiling, and head back to my car.

Things are starting to look up. I can feel it in my heart, it still hurts but it beats on. When one life ends, it should not mean that others end as well. I am so lucky to have these people in my life. I startup my car, now, time for some much needed sleep.

Chapter 13

$\mathcal{G}$raduation is fast approaching. In just two days, I will be leaving this school and entering the real world. The real world, can you imagine? It has only been a week since I made things right with everyone.

I told Zac that I was not ready for a relationship, but our friendship still means the world to me. I mean, we have forever to figure it out. Emily and I talked for hours on everything that I had held in throughout the last couple of months. She was the only therapy I needed, damn the doctors.

I have slowly began to transition into the world once more, I refuse to waste another minute of my Senior year. I am still heartbroken over the loss of my best friend and soulmate, but life keeps spinning on whether you want it to or not. It is better to get spun up in life, than let it whirl on past me.

I watch the principal put my name on the record board next to the previous record holder, a record she held for nine years before I entered the scheme of things. I am standing proudly next to my friends as she calls me up for the honorary photo next to the board. I smile brightly as the camera goes off. As the flash continues going off, I have an idea for graduation.

I run to my friends after the photo op, "Guys, I have an idea for graduation!"

Samantha beams at me, always one for a good idea, "what is it?"

"We make t-shirts with Byron on them and wear them, to include him in our ceremony. What do you think?" I eagerly search their faces, wanting approval for a way to mourn my friend in a healthy manner. I happily see them look as excited as me at the proposal.

"That is a great idea, Ella! Then we can unzip our gowns at the end when we toss up our caps!" Tara claps her hand, an idea forming in her head. Samantha and Emily squeal in response.

"Yes, that is perfect. I will make the shirts and give them out to the class, plus anyone else who wants them." I chime back in, excited for the upcoming events. Excited for the first time in months when thinking of my deceased love.

"I think it is a great idea as well." Zac steps in from his area behind my girl-friends. I laugh at seeing him emerge from behind us gabby girls.

"It is settled then, lets get started." Emily states. "We can all help!"

I smile, "I need to start getting on that speech of mine. Graduation speeches aren't really something you wing, are they?"

"No, I think not." Emily agrees, while rolling her eyes at me. I laugh at her response. My happiness slowly returning, leaving only the hole that Byron left.

"You guys ready to head to exams?" I say. Exams are today. Most of the Seniors have their exams scheduled on the same day, I unfortunately have one tomorrow also. So I will be one of the last seniors in school.

"Ella, have you forgotten about Senior auction?" Samantha tuts me.

Oh my gosh, Senior auction. I had completely forgotten. Before exams start on the Seniors last day, an auction is held to raise money for the senior trip. I also forgot to mention the senior trip we take the day before graduation. Our last couple days are jam packed. So many things I have forgotten in my haze of depression and self hate.

Firstly, senior auction is where the seniors sign up to let themselves be bid upon by the underclassmen. Whoever bids the largest amount, gets to order the senior around all day as they follow them around. We call it senior servant day, it is a way for the seniors to raise money and for the underclassmen to have some fun.

"Crap, I guess so. When is it?" I ask.

"In like five minutes." Tara laughs at me.

"What? Why hasn't anyone told me?"

"We have. You were just busy in Ella Land like usual. Do you even know where our Senior trip is being held?"

I shake my head no. I had not really planned on caring about any of this stuff.

Samantha sighs, "We are all going to Cedar Point, pay attention Ella! Good thing you have friends like us, and we worry about this for you. By the way, you are being paired with me for the senior auction and Emily is with Tara. Same for graduation walks."

Samantha tells me what is going on before I even have time to process it. Wow, I have missed a lot. I know that I am only paired with Sam because she will get a high bid with or without me, I mean who would want a mopey girl unless she was a package deal with the most popular girl in school?

"Now, lets go get ready for our auctioning!" Tara giggles, and we head to the gym.

"When are exams then?" I ask, still thinking about my upcoming exam.

Emily sighs at me, "They are after the auction. Then tomorrow we come back to be servants to whomever purchased us. Then the next day is our senior trip, and graduation is two days after that. Don't you pay attention?"

"I guess not." I chuckle at her.

"Ladies, come on!" Samantha says as she heads towards the gym. I look around for Zac, and realize he must have bailed before our conversation even started. Sneaky kid, I didn't even notice, but I guess I don't notice a lot anymore. I chuckle once more to myself, what a haze I have been in. Thank god for good friends. I turn to head to the gym with my wonderful friends.

"NEXT UP, SAMANTHA AND ELLA. START THE BIDDING." The principal announces us, waiting for the hands to raise. My friends must have stuck me with Samantha because they were worried that no one would want to purchase me, but with her, every underclassmen male will want to try to win her for the day.

"$5!"

"$10!"

"$12!"

"$15!"

The bidding rarely goes above $20, not many are that dedicated to purchase a servant, but I would not be surprised if the bidding goes higher with Sam. Everyone that has bidded so far is an underclassmen male. Called it.

"$50!" A shout comes from the sophomores. Hushed whispers go around, and no one ups the bidder. I look to see who it is. I see my little brother waving his hand in the air, his friends laughing at his side.

"THE HIGHEST BID GOES TO REESE!" She shouts, pointing at Reese. My little brother smiles triumphantly and looks right at me, smirking. That little bastard.

Samantha is laughing at my side, "Looks like we have it in for us." She says to me.

"I guess we do." I reply, and laugh with her, never losing eye contact with my sibling. I guess someone wanted me after all.

When the auction ends, I exit the gymnasium and head to my locker for the stuff for my first exam. Zac is already waiting for me by my locker.

"I see your little brother bought you." He jeers at my predicament. A sibling buying you in high school is quite the fate. They have no obligation to not humiliating you. Actually, they find joy in it. I know my little brother sure will.

"Yes, he did indeed. You didn't feel like joining the auction?" I had noticed that Zac was not one of the seniors up for bidding.

He shakes his head, "Nah, I mean, I figured the girls would be tearing their clothes off for me, and I couldn't handle that." He winks at me, and I laugh at him. Always the wise guy.

"Well, I need to head to my first exam. I will talk to you afterward."

"Oops, forgot you have to get their early or you will explode!"

"Shut up." I shove him, and head to my class. It feels good to get back in the way of things. I have missed the jesting and the laughing, I missed smiling most. Smiling is like a drug, it warms up your heart and leaves a happy feeling in your chest, it is contagious also. Once it happens, it spreads throughout your body like the best kind of magic.

Byron. There it is again. The voice at the back of my head reminding me that someone is missing this. I think of him, and how he would have been on the sidelines with Zac at the auction. Or, maybe Jerry and Rick would have forced him into it. So many different outcomes that could have been, instead he wasn't here. I will be damned if he gets left out though, I begin to think about the shirts I am going to create.

I am still thinking about the options, when the teacher says pencils out, and my first exam begins.

"Thank God all my exams are over! I am a free woman! Well, today anyways."
Emily approaches my locker after school.

"Man, I still have one tomorrow morning. Calculus. I hope I do alright,
considering I no longer have a tutor." I try not to frown at the thought.

"Don't you dare do that, Ella. I am sure you will do great, besides, you can't
lose your spot or anything. No worries!" She pats me on the back.

"Yeah, yeah. I suppose not."

"Get some good sleep, I bet your little bro has a lot planned for you!" She
laughs at me, as I swat her with my folders. I shut my locker and head out to the
car, where I see Reese waiting for me with his friend, Eric.

"Hey sis, ready for tomorrow!" My little brothers smiles at me, and his
friend laughs.

I smile back, "Just remember I am your ride, little bro."

"Oh, I know! Don't worry I won't be that bad, besides, I am sharing you
girls with Eric. You think I just had $50?"

I look at Eric, "don't make me do anything stupid, and I won't make your
life hell."

Eric laughs at me, "don't worry, I will take that death threat with a grain of
salt." Reese snorts. Eric has always been one of my favorites of Reese's friends.

"Okay, I take it I am taking you two somewhere?" I beckon them to the car.

"Yeah, wanna drop us off at Eric's? His car is broken, so he needs a ride."

I nod my head, "K, sure. Hope in."

We all clamber into my vehicle.

After I am home, I get onto my computer to start making the shirts for graduation. I settle on a cheaper site, and search for a photo of Byron. My chest begins
to constrict as I search the photos of us, and him, until I find the right one. A
picture of Byron I snapped of him at a party the summer before our Senior year.

He is smiling at the camera, smiling at me. I remember taking this.

"Byron, smile for the camera!" I shout at him over the music.

*He turns to me, and frowns, "No way, I hate pictures!" He holds his hand up, blurring
the picture I was attempting.*

"Byron, will you please just let you best friend snap memories of you? How hard can it be?"

His frown deepens, "Must you pull that crap?"

I laugh at his frustrations, "Of course! And, besides you look adorable. Especially with that tipsy look in your eye." I tease him, and he rolls his eyes at me.

"I am not tipsy!" He bellows at me, obviously offended. Then, he tilts back too far in his chair and falls backwards. I hold in my laugh, and rush to help him up.

"Not tipsy, huh?"

"Shut up, Ella." He can't help but begin to laugh.

I take that moment to pick up my camera, "There it is!" I snap the picture as he stares back at me, laughing together.

My flashback brings emotions flooding back to the surface. How I miss Byron. I would like to think that knowing the pain he caused, maybe he would have changed his mind. Perhaps, he was lost in a moment of grief and forgot about the consequences.

No. It doesn't help to hope. He is gone, and that is that. I click on the picture, blowing up his face as he smiled at me.

I quickly design the shirts, settling for a quote on the back by Emily Dickinson, "unable are the loved to die, for love is immortality." Her poems have always found a way into my heart, and this one seems to fit perfectly.

I order the shirts, and close the page. Enough sulking for one day, my next task is to concentrate on my speech. I have not even started it yet. There are so many things that I could include in my speech, and I think I know where to start.

I turn up the radio, and begin to write once more. Instead of holding back the tears as I wrote the other, I hold back my smile as I write about my high school experiences. It amazes me the way that writing can hold such powerful emotion, I suppose it makes sense though, it is one of the most powerful forms of expression.

Well, today my little brother is my master. Anyways, that is what he has informed Samantha and I we must begin calling him and Eric. So far, we have just been following them around all day, carrying their books and wearing odd clothes.

My little brother kindly dismissed me for my only exam of the day, but demanded that I be back directly afterward for our "makeovers." I almost regret letting my friends sweep me up into this nonsense, almost. Our makeovers consisted of dressing us in old bathrobes and wearing crowns. He wanted to put his version of makeup on us, but Samantha gave him the look where he decided against it.

"Do you think he is going to make us do anything silly for lunch?" Samantha whispers to me as we trail after Reese and Eric.

"Yeah, probably. I mean, it is my little brother and his best friend. They have no conscience, they simply want to make us look as stupid as possible." I say back to her matter of factly. In our lunch room, we have a stage set up, it is actually a lunch/theatre. The perks of having a poor country school is we like to combine things to make it cheaper. We also have a workout room in an old bus garage, I have to admit, we make things work.

Anyways, on Senior servant day, some of the more wicked "masters" have their servants get on the stage to sing, recite a play, dance, etc. I know that Reese has something planned, I just don't know what it is yet, but I know that I am about to find out.

"Okay, ladies, you ready for lunch?" Reese turns to face us, his lopsided grin growing as we approach the lunch room. Oh gosh.

"Yes, Master." We both say at once, Samantha trying to control her sputtering of a laughter building up. She has trouble saying the master part, it is too much for her drama queen persona.

"Great! Eric you get to tell me sister what she needs to do, and I will inform Samantha of hers." Eric's eyes flutter over to me, and he tries to re enact Reese's malicious grin, but fails. Eric is too nice for this, Reese was playing it safe with me by allowing him to tell me what to do at lunch.

"How come she gets Eric?!" Samantha whines.

"Did I hear some backtalk?" Reese tuts at her, and she glares at the back of my little brother's head as he turns away. "To the cafeteria!"

Reese and Samantha begin walking away, as Eric stands still, looking down at his feet. Poor kid probably doesn't know what to do with me.

"Well, are we going?" I ask him.

He looks up, almost alarmed that I am still here, "uhh, yeah." But he doesn't move. His confidence drained once my brother left him alone with me.

"Aww, someone not sure how to handle me when not around my brother? In that case, I don't think that you should have me do anything on that silly stage, how about you give me a break so I can go sit with my friends? I have had a long day. Please?" I look up at him (he is quite tall for an underclassman) and give him my best puppy dog eyes.

His face melts, I have him, Reese didn't think this one through. "Man, I don't know, Reese kind of wants me to have you do something there. He would be pretty annoyed with me if I just let you off..."

"Eric, come on. I am just exhausted from all of this, it takes a lot out of me nowadays. I have had a rough year, yah know?"

His uncertainty intensifies, "Ella, I know what you are doing. But, sorry, you are going to get on that stage and I am going to have you dance to the song of my choosing."

He attempts to stand his ground, but his voice tells the truth.

"Eric, please don't make me... You have always been my favorite of Reese's friends." I end my sentence by throwing my arms around him for a hug.

He is too stunned to move, then of all things, he hugs me back. "Okay, Ella, you can go sit with you friends. You win."

I step back, and smile brightly at him, I had won. "Thank you, Eric! You are the best!" I stand on my tip toes, and lightly kiss him on the cheek. His cheeks flush, they turn the same color as his shirt. Funny boy he is, it is like he has had no interaction with girls, which I guess he probably hasn't. Reese is going to kill him for letting me weasel my way around performing.

"Yeah, yeah. Go away before Reese comes out to kill me." He smiles sheepishly at me, and I turn to walk towards the cafeteria, leaving him standing alone in the hall. I see him touching his cheek as I turn the corner.

I triumphantly stride into the lunch room, and sit with my friends. The ones whose masters don't make them do as much.

"I take it you guys didn't have much senior servant duties today?" I sit by Tara and Emily.

They shake their heads, "Nah, Rebecca bought us just to carry her books, we have had it quite nice!" Tara laughs.

"Yep, I think she only bought us because Tara snapped at her at that party back in the beginning of the year." Emily chides in.

"And, she only wanted to talk about Byron." Tara says, as Emily quickly jabs her with her elbow. "Ow! What? Ella is a big girl, we can say his name. Right, El?" They both turn to see my reaction, I hold in the sadness threatening to flood my face.

"Yeah, you can mention him. I am fine, of course Rebecca would want to talk about him. They were friends!"

"See? Told you." Tara sticks her tongue out at Emily, and Emily sticking hers out in retaliation.

"You guys are dumb." I snicker at them.

"Uh oh, looks like your master is headed this way, Ella!" Emily points, and I see Reese heading my way. Crap.

He stands in front of my table, arms crossed, and I see Eric come up behind him, looking at me apologetically.

"How dare you flirt your way out of your performance!" Reese says to me.

"What? I did no such thing." I feign ignorance, and my friends laugh.

"You did too!"

"Did not!"

"Did too!"

"Whatever. I am not going to fight with you like a child."

Eric takes this moment to butt in, "I just thought she had enough for the day, you said I was in charge of her, so that is that."

My little brother rolls his eyes at Eric, and replies, "Ugh, fine." Then bumps him as he returns back to his table with Samantha who had been behind him the entire time, her eyes begging us to pity her.

Once again, Eric stands back awkwardly, I decide to save him. "You can sit with us until my little bro isn't being such a jerk." I say, and motion for him to sit next to us.

"No, I am okay, but umm thanks, Ella." He turns red once more, and walks away from our table.

"Aww!! Looks like someone has a little crush on you!" Tara teases me.

"The little brother's friend, I like it." Emily laughs.

"Shut up!" I giggle at them, blushing at their accusations.

"Hey, it is just nice to see you smiling again and besides, he is absolutely adorable."

"What? No! I just didn't feel like getting on the stage. He is Reese's FRIEND." I jump in, defending my honor.

"Okay, okay. Fine! But he is probably one of the cutest underclassmen, just saying. You choose them right, you cradle robber." Emily winks at me, as Tara begins rolling with laughter.

"I hate you guys." I say as I begin giggling too.

"Yeah, sure you do!" Tara laughs at me.

"Woah, did I miss something?" Zac comes up to the table, placing his tray down and looking at us. Which makes us laugh even harder.

"Ella! Wake up!"

"WAKEY, WAKEY!"

What the? I slowly open my eyes to see Tara, Emily, and Samantha bouncing on my bed.

"What are you people doing here?" I whine at them, collapsing back onto my bed.

"Umm, we are going to Cedar Point today, duh!" Samantha squeals at me.

I turn to my clock, 7:13 am. "Why are you here so early?" I whine again.

"Because the bus leaves at 8, and we knew you wouldn't remember! We already grabbed you some McDonalds, now get up!" Emily starts pushing me into an upwards position.

"You know, I love you guys, but I hate you too." I mumble as I start getting up to get dressed. "And, you are lucky that I do not sleep naked." They are also lucky that my nightmares of Byron have began to calm down, waking me up during one of those could have been disastrous.

My friends ignore me, and begin talking about the trip today. It turns out I really knew nothing about this trip, my mind being too preoccupied with sorrow and Byron in the last few months. I really had let it control my life...

The bus leaves at 8 am (figured that out), we are all riding together, and we will get there around noon, staying until 8 pm. We will not get back until late tonight, and my friends are already prepared with alcohol. They may have told me other important aspects of the trip, but my mind is still muddled from my rude awakening.

"Are you ready YET? It is almost 8!" Emily's voice drags me out of my own thoughts.

"What? Yeah. Where is the McDonalds?" I am so hungry.

"Haha, typical. Once we get you into the car, it is all yours." Tara waggles her finger at me, and I sigh, grabbing my things to follow them to Sam's car.

"Okay, let's go." I mumble, throwing my bag over my shoulder.

"Yay!" My friends cheer, and we trample down the stairs.

The bus ride was obnoxious, that many teenagers should not be allowed to be in such a compact space for over three hours.

My friends insisted on beginning their day drinking, as I scarfed down my McMuffin they had retrieved for me. I did not feel the need to begin my day drinking on the bus, I mean, I want to go on the rides without barfing. I had also noticed that drinking only brings the memories of Byron back to me since the last time I drank was with him, and for my last few days of highschool, I did not want to dwell on the painful past.

I have to admit I am quite excited for Cedar Point. I went there a couple of times with my family when I was younger, but I haven't been since I grew up. Nor have I ever been with my friends.

We are finally here, my wristband is on and I am ready to experience the park.

"Ready for some rides?" Zac appears by my side, having sat by him on the bus, we decided it would be the most fun if we went on the rides together. My friends will not make it long considering they are already slurring their words, they may need a nap by the end of the day.

I smile into the warm sun, "oh yes, I am quite ready."

The day speeds on by, the length of lines does not even lower my excitement throughout the day. The roller coasters and rides are exhilarating. Tara, Sam, and Emily try to keep up with me throughout the day, but as I expected, the alcohol catches up to them and they decide upon naps beneath a pavilion they find.

"You lazy bums!" I jeer at them, as they wave me away and settle in on their benches.

"Go on without us, Ella! We will find you later." Emily yawns, and stretches onto her bench. It does not look comfortable at all, but they seem to not care.

"Looks like we have the rest of the days to ourselves." Zac's grin is contagious, I can't help but smile up at him.

"That is the way it looks."

"Want to go on the Millennium Force again?"

"Only if we can race on the Gemini again afterward."

"It's on."

We head to the Millennium Force, the line looking shorter than it did earlier in the day. People must be starting to wane, it is quite hot for a late spring day.

"Are you having fun?" Zac asks me.

I don't even have to think about it before I respond, "Oh my gosh, yes. This is the most fun that I have had in a while!" And I mean it.

Zac looks down at me, "I am so glad to hear you say that."

"Are you having fun?" I ask him in return.

"More than you could imagine." He replies softly, looking deep into my eyes. I can feel the pressure of our relationship or whatever it is we have going on, building to the surface.

"Zac…" I begin, but he cuts me down.

"Nope, no serious talk today, my Ella. Today, is just for fun! So, don't even start with that nonsense. We can talk about anything we need to after graduation, I mean, we will have all summer. But for now, I just want you to have the perfect day like prom." He winks at me, and I blush.

"Sounds good to me." I laugh at him. He is so perfect, I wish that give him the love that he so deserves. Byron. The name pops into my mind, then his face, his memory. I begin to pick at the memory, trying not to dwell.

"Our turn!" Zac screams at me, breaking me from the oncoming trance. Just in time. I have my entire life to mourn the loss of my best friend, and just now to enjoy my only senior trip.

"Woo! Lets go!" I cry, grabbing his hand and dragging him onto the ride, smiling all the way.

"Oh my gosh, I am so tired." I exclaim, it must be close to 8pm by now. I check my watch, 7:00.

"Well, according to your watch, we still have about an hour before the bus leaves." Zac says. "Any last minute ride you would like to go on?"

"Hmm, I know!" He smiles at me, and I lead him to the the colorful carousel that we had passed numerous times, but never ridden.

"The merry go round, huh? Letting that little kid in you get out, I see." He chuckles at me as I point to the bright blue spotted carriage being lead by a hot pink unicorn as my riding choice. He sits in the carriage and pats the seat next to him. "Care to join me, miss?"

"Why, don't mind if I do!" I pretend curtsy to him, and gracefully plop down beside him. I relax as the carousel begins to spin around, the music chirping brightly at us.

"Now, why is this your last ride choice? If you don't mind me asking." He turns and asks me.

"No, I don't mind. I chose it because it reminds me of childhood. I loved riding it as a kid, my dad used to insist that I only ride the ones that had seatbelts in them, securing me to whatever animal I chose. That is what childhood is, being safe and secure, letting your parents take care of you. And now? I can ride the carousel without a seatbelt, I can choose whatever creature I want to. The options are infinite, I can choose anyone of them, but that also takes away my safety belt. It means that I am free to make my own choices, but not all of them are the safe route."

I finish my speech to see Zac leaning towards me and he kisses me. I kiss him back, letting it linger, letting myself feel his lips on mine. The spark still there even after all we have been through together.

We pull apart, and Zac says, "You are amazing. You take even the smallest insignificant things, and create something beautiful out of them. Your mind works in such wonderful ways, Ella. How can I not fall in love with you?"

I laugh at him, "You mean me turning the carousel into a metaphor about growing up is hot?"

"Oh, so hot." He teases me, and then gets serious once more. "Your take on the world, it's beautiful. I just hope you see that." Then his seriousness breaks, the music ending, the ride slowly coming to a stop. "Well, it looks like you chose the route with no safety, miss Ella. Now, it is time for you to leave your childhood behind."

He says it jokingly, but in all reality, getting off this carousel was leaving my childhood behind. We were going to graduate in two days, join the real world, become a part of society. The senior trip is a way of getting a final goodbye to the life you had lived for so long.

"Guess so! To the bus." I can't stop smiling, finally looking forward to what life has in store for me.

By the time we get to the bus, everyone has already boarded, waiting on us. My friends are wide awake, having slept the day away. We walk to the back of the bus.

"You guys finally ready to join the big kids and party?" Colin is sitting next to Samantha, holding up a water bottle (I am assuming not filled with water like usual). I shake my head at my friends, and grab the bottle from Colin. Time to say the last time I drank was with my friends on our senior trip, replacing a sad memory with a happy one.

"Lets go." I whoop into the air as my friends begin to cheer and the bus slowly pulls away from Cedar Point. I am too busy with my friends to even notice it fade away into the darkness.

Chapter 14

*T*oday is graduation day. My family has been fretting around all day, making last minute adjustments to my post graduation party that is taking place right after the ceremony. We are having it outside, and my mother went through a lot to have everything set up in time. Byron's mother has been setting up a spot for Byron's memorial as well. I try not to dwell on the fact that something is missing from today.

She catches me staring at her from my bedroom window, and waves at me, smiling, the smile never reaching her eyes. She was happy that I asked her if she would like to set up a memorial, but I know that today is not going to a happy event for her. I wave back, and turn away from the window.

I am all ready for the ceremony. I am wearing my Byron shirt, they came in the mail just in time. I plan on handing them out before the ceremony to everyone who ordered one. I am nervous, I have not rehearsed my speech at all, nor have I told my parents and friends the college I chose yet. I am planning on surprising them at the end of my speech.

I am lost in thought as my mother storms into my room, "Ella! Are you ready? You have to be there an hour early, remember?" Then she stops, and looks at me.

I am wearing my Byron shirt over a sleek white dress that I had chosen before my idea for the shirts. With my shirt it simply looks like a cute skirt. I have also straightened my hair, and pinned it back from my face. My gown is draping over my chair, ready to be thrown on. I can see my mother's eyes welling up with tears.

"Oh, my little baby is growing up so fast." She whimpers at me.

"Moooom, don't you dare."

"No, no. You are right! Don't worry, I will not cry. Not yet anyway. I am just so proud of you." She pats at her eyes with her shirt, and sniffles. "Now, throw on that gown and go! You can't be late for your own party." She laughs at her own joke and ushers me to the door. "Don't worry about the box of shirts, I will have Reese grab them so you don't wrinkle your gown. REESE!"

My little brother's head appears in my doorway, "What?"

"Get that box for your sister and bring it to the car."

"Ugh, what about John?"

"John is helping me set up downstairs, GO!" She uses her mom voice and the argument is settle. Reese leans down, and picks up the box.

"Thanks, Reeses Pieces." My mom croons at him, I can hear him mumble under his breath as he carries the box down the stairs for me.

"Ella. Didn't I say GO?" My mom looks to see me still standing there, and I rush down the stairs after my little brother. Time for me to go graduate.

"Okay, okay. Everybody line up!" Emily and I take our places in line, deciding last minute that we had to walk together. Being best friends and all. The teachers helping us out all begin to usher us into neat rows of two, I am at the front of the line behind the Valedictorian and his walking partner.

I try not to think about how Byron and I should be the two at the beginning of the line.

"Sooo, since we are both going to be Valedictorian this year…" I begin, nonchalantly as Byron and I are sitting together outside my grandpa's house swinging on the swing as we take a break from our homework.

"I take it you are about to ask me if I want to walk together?" Byron interrupts me before I can even ask.

I harumph at him, "Way to ruin it for me."

He chuckles at me, always chuckling at me. I am almost proud that I am one of the few who gets to see this beautiful boy shine when he laughs. A rare thing for this quiet kid.

"You are predictable, Ella. But don't worry, I love that about you. And yes, we can walk together. I figured you would have already asked me by now." He smirks at me, nudging me with his elbow.

"If you knew so well, how come you didn't ask me?!" I ask, offended that he called me predictable.

"Because, I figured it would be better if you asked. Not my job in this friendship."

"You hardly have a job in this friendship, you lazy friend."

"Hey, who is helping you with math right now?"

"No one, my math book is inside."

"Always such a wise girl."

"Wise girl?"

"Yeah, wise guy, but since you are a girl. Yah know?"

"Oh, I get it, just wanted to hear you explain it." I take this moment to shove him off the swing, and jump off gracefully behind him.

"How old are you?!" He cries at me, brushing the dirt off of his pants, that are now dirty from his ungraceful fall.

"Ummm, old enough?" I laugh at him.

"Walk by yourself!" He yells, throwing grass clumps at me. He gets up, and begins walking towards me, grass clumps in hand.

"Don't you dare, Byron. Grass stains are impossible to get out, and I really like these jeans." I say, backing up cautiously.

"Should have thought about that." He says, and continues towards me, and I break out into a run with him close behind me, screaming all the way.

I feel a hand on my shoulder. "Don't think about him, Ella. Today is your day, and you are allowing everyone to remember him too. Keep your head up, and don't mess up on your speech." Emily pep talks me next to me, as we all begin our walk to our seats.

"Thanks, Em." I attempt smiling at her, the lump still in my throat. The memory too fresh in my mind to forget it just yet.

We make our way to our seats, and the principal begins the introduction to our ceremony. The gymnasium is packed with people, friends and families of everyone here. It is beginning to get sticky in here from the overwhelming heat coming from the bodies of so many people. I look up and search for my family. I don't look too long before I see them in the upper right hand corner of the bleachers, they wave at me. I smile at them, and go back to listening to the principal.

"Now, first we will hear from the Salutatorian." Crap. I forgot that I speak first, I guess I should have paid more attention when I was being told what to do. "Please welcome to the podium, Ella Cane." I hear the clapping, and Emily pushes me up from my seat.

"Go get 'em, Tiger." I nod my head, and head to the podium.

"Hello, my name is Ella Cane." I begin, and then stop, my speech, where is it? I fumble through my pockets and realize that I must have left it in my car. Everyone is staring at me, my palms begin to fill with sweat. I guess, this is where I have to wing it, I smile, Byron would be shaking his head at me right now knowing exactly what I had done.

With his memory floating in my mind, I begin my speech.

"Ahem. Well, I guess the best way to start this off, is congratulations class of 2010! It seems like such a short while ago that I was just entering high school as a freshman, all nervous and excited to enter the big bad high school that my brother was always talking about. I mean I knew that this was where it was at, this is where everything was happening. This is the place that homecoming went on, dances, prom, all that awesome stuff, I was pumped.

I thought that when I entered high school, I would just grow up and become someone completely new. I was going to make a ton of new friends, I was going to get more mature, grow a few inches, and do all the things that my brother talked about... And, you know what? All of those things did happen, but at a much slower pace than what I had initially expected.

I didn't just automatically grow up like I thought I would, my freshman year I was just a kid. My friends and I had so many things that we had to learn, most of them were learned the hard way.

In school, I learned a lot of lessons, some more important than others. I mean yeah, I learned the typical things you learn in school like math, english, science and all of that, but I am talking about the lessons that you will remember forever. Here are the the top three lessons that I will keep with me forever.

The first thing that I learned is, that if you have a good friend that will always be there for you, then you have to be there for them to, especially when they need you the most. Even if one of your friends makes a mistake, you need to be there for them to wipe their tears, because when that time comes around for you, they will be there. We are all human, and mistakes happen, we learn to forgive, especially if that person is important to you.

Number two, is that people change, it happens. We can't get mad at them, or ask them to change back. You simply have to accept it, or go your separate ways. Everyone changes, especially as we are growing up, it is a part of life. I don't think that a single person is the same exact person they were their freshman year.

And the third most important lesson I learned is that if you care about someone, you need to tell them. I am not talking about the, oh I like you kind of care, but the kind of caring that you have for someone that you have known forever. The kind of care that you have for a good friend that means a lot to you. Someone that has helped you become who you are today, someone who has been there for you the whole time. Now, is the perfect time for this, a lot of our classmates we may never see again, and after 13 years of going to the same school with these people, why not?

High school teaches you the the things that you need to know when you enter the real world. It teaches you to be a better person and to be who you want to be because someone is always going to disapprove no matter what. Going into high school isn't what makes you an adult, it is what you learn and accomplish in those four years that make you who you are today.

With that final lesson, I would like to thank all of my friends for sticking with me after all of these years... I want to thank my parents for supporting me in everything that I do and letting me by my own person. I want to thank Tara, Samantha, and Emily for always making it to my breakfasts, even when they dwindled this past year. I also want to thank Byron Rood, even though he is no longer with us. He was my motivation for being up here right now, and I wish he was here with me.

With that, I would like to announce that I am going to The University of Michigan to study Journalism this Fall, thank you and good bye."

I take that moment to look up, and smile at the crowd. My friends begin cheering, everyone stands, and for a fleeting moment, everything is alright in the world. Byron made me realize that life is too short to not pursue your passion, and I am going to share my stories with the world.

I make my way back to my seat with my friends patting me on the back, and Pete (the Valedictorian) makes his way to the podium for his speech.

"Great speech, El." Emily whispers to me.

"Thanks." I whisper back as Pete begins talking. His speech is similar to mine, but more about the quality of a good school system. His speech sounds robotic.

I hear a tap on my shoulder, and Zac leans up to my ear, "Michigan, huh? Looks like the fates are on our side, Miss Ella." I want to turn around him and ask where he is going, but a stern look from Emily to stop my talking makes me wait.

As Pete continues his speech, I begin thinking about the past year. The ups and the downs. I would never have become the person that I am if everything had not happened as it did. Thinking of how Byron could have been here makes my chest constrict. His smile, his eyes, I miss them. I miss everything about him.

The memories are still overwhelming, but they do not suffocate me as they once did. Emily sees me, and reaches over to squeeze my hand. My friends saved me from the pain that I allowed to suffocate me for so many months. Byron made a mistake, he chose not to turn to his friends with his problems and they broke him. I learned from him, and I did not let that same path consume me.

I hear applause as Pete's speech ends, I applaud as well, feeling guilty that I did not pay attention at all.

The names for our diplomas begin getting called, I am up third, right behind Pete and his friend. Emily squeezes my hand again, as we begin our ascent to the stage.

"Ella Cane." I hear my name, and I walk up to the stage. I see my dad attempting to get a good angle as he approaches the stage with his camera. The principal shakes my hand and congratulates me as she hands me the diploma. "Congratulations, Ella." She says.

"Thank you." I reply, and begin my descent as I hear Emily's name being called.

"Smile, Princess!" My dad yells at me as I exit the stage, I turn towards him and cheese, with my diploma in my hand.

Soon, everyone's name is called, and I look to Emily.

"We did it." I smile, I cannot control my happiness.

"We did." She says.

"Congratulations class of 2010!" We all cheer and throw our caps up into the air, and unzip our gowns, proudly showing our missing classmates face. The entire gym is in an uproar, we did it. My friends all gather around me.

"We are official high school graduates!" Samantha beams at me.

"Yes!" Tara cries.

I look around at the faces of all of my friends, smiling and crying at the same time. This is what life is for, it is for these little moments. Even when life gets you down, and every corner is filled with sadness, there is still a light at every turn.

Byron had forgotten about these moments we live for in this painful life. He let the pain of the world consume him, he was not ready to face the world head on. He would forever remain a 17 year old, unable to grow up.

He did not see the light shining from his friend's faces, only the fear of growing up and the darkness that awaited him outside these doors. He had lost his battle, and I had failed him. I know this, but I will not make that mistake again. I was still a child when I lost my best friend, but I have emerged an adult.

Someday, the world will know his story, I promise him that. My friend, forever 17, it is time to let you go. You created the person I am today, and for that I am eternally thankful, but I think that I am finally ready to grow up and face any challenge that lay ahead.

Epilogue

I guess that this story wasn't really about Byron, but about me. This was my story about how the world lost a shining star. How it fell from the skies, leaving only destruction in it's wake. Byron's decision affected everyone around him, leaving a crater that no one could fill.

He took his family and friends down with him. We fell into the crater he left behind and we were forced to climb our way out of it. Byron was never meant to be here. He flew through the night, and when he crashed, he left a mark that would never leave the people he touched. He would forever live on in the lives of the people who loved him.

I suppose you are all wondering what happened afterwards right? Well, it turns out that Zac was also going to Michigan. The irony, right? The fates were finally on my side. I guess happy endings do exist. Our love wasn't the kind that struck like a match, nor the kind that would make for a great love story, but it was our story. Zac held onto me, and breathed life into me when I thought that all was gone.

Zac got a track scholarship there, and is studying Exercise Science. He wants to be a coach. I am studying Journalism, so that I can share people's stories with the world. Byron gave me courage to follow my own path, not the one that was laid out for me, but one that I created myself. I found love, even in the darkness.

Now, lets see. Tara and Samantha chose to go to the local community college; we still keep in touch. Emily got accepted into Michigan State, so she is officially my rival. We skype on a regular basis. I will always remember my friends who gave me hope. True friends who stood by my side.

My life kept spinning after I lost Byron. I suppose that is life though. It doesn't care who you are, it will continue on without you. As I get older, I understand that Byron must not have truly understood the consequences of his actions. I mean, how can you when you are only 17 and the only life you have ever lived was inside a small town?

Byron was a beautiful, dark star that fell from the skies too quickly. He was perfect, but he could not see his own perfection. All he saw were his flaws, and what was wrong. He was not ready to grow up, nor ready to challenge the world head on.

I would like to think that he has once again found himself among the stars. This life was not ready for him, but perhaps the next one will be.

He took a piece of my soul with him that day he left, and it will always be there. Time heals, but it does not make you forget. Some wounds will never close, you simply learn to live with them, they become a part of who you are.

Byron changed me. His actions made me realize my own strength. In times of pain, you realize how strong you can truly be. I fell down, I broke apart in his absence, but I learned from it. I learned that you cannot let the pain consume you, because there is no such thing as darkness, darkness is only the absence of light. You need to find your light, and let it shine through the darkness.

There are many signs of depression and suicide, but as a teenager, they are easily dismissed. Mistaken for teen angst, so many teenagers die every year from suicide. Don't let this happen to your loved one. Remember, suicide affects more than one life. Learn from my story; from Byron; and show them that with every stumble, there is a way to get back up again.

Byron was an oddity placed upon this earth, and now, he will forever be my fallen star.

Although this story was based on a true story, I chose to give Ella choices and chances that I never had. I hope that sharing Byron's story will show others that depression and suicide affect more than just one life. You can find your light through the darkness, you just need to keep fighting.

About the Author

Hannah Reuter (H.B. Catherine) was raised in the small town of Marcellus, Michigan. She graduated from Western Michigan University and is currently writing more books. She loves travelling, playing her guitar, and reading. If you would like to find out more about her upcoming books, and read about her campaign to bring more awareness to suicide and depression, check out her website at www.hbcatherinewriting.com.

Made in the USA
Middletown, DE
18 February 2016